Omegaverse Terms

A few things to know regarding the omegaverse world. The people in the omegaverse display a more canine or wolflike behavior. Some books involve shifting into wolves. This series will have minimal shifting.

Here are some terms that will be helpful to know (*note: these definitions pertain to my stories and not all omegaverse stories):

Omega: A female or male who would often have multiple partners to help them during heats. Usually has a particular scent that alphas find very appealing and unable to resist.

Beta: Like a normal human in the wolf world

Alpha: Top of the food chain, and they gravitate to omegas. They also have a scent that attracts omegas.

Delta: Ferocious and deadly

Slick: Secretion from the privates

Heat: A period where an omega needs to mate - akin to ovulating in human females.

Knot: When an alpha mates and omega, and the base of the penis swells, locking the alpha and omega in place.

Rut: Alphas can go into rut phase, similar to heat. Sometimes an omega's heat will bring it on.

Scent blockers: Can come in pills or as a cream. Blocks an omega scent from attracting alphas.

Heat Suppressants: Stops an omega from going into heat

Content Guide

If you don't have any triggers, please skip this page to avoid any spoilers! For any questions regarding triggers, please email: author_laylasparks@yahoo.com

~ Double Penetration
   ~ Menage
   ~ Group Play
   ~ Backdoor (anal) play
   ~ Kidnapping (pleasuring, edging)
   ~ Pregnancy (mention of it)
   ~ Domestic Discipline/ Spanking
   ~ Claiming bites

Prologue

Lacy

Raindrops pelted against the window as I cuddled under the blankets with my alpha boyfriend, Jordan.

I never thought it would be my last night with him.

At the sound of the thunderstorm ripping through the night sky, I hugged him tighter, and he smiled, pressing his lips to mine. I'd known Jordan for three months now after meeting him during my freshman year in college.

I leaned into his embrace, resting my head on his chest, feeling the steady beat of his heart against my ear. His cologne mingled with the earthy scent of rain from the open window, creating a sensory haven.

His hand ventured lower to my butt, and I froze.

"Not yet," I said softly. I watched the lines on his jaw tense, and I could sense his energy changing as the seconds ticked by.

He wasn't happy.

He hadn't even introduced me to his pack yet, but I wasn't ready even if he did. I was nineteen, and I wanted my first knotting to be special.

"Lacy, I know you're scared. But sex with an alpha isn't all

1

that scary, I promise," said Jordan, sighing. "It's been three months already. Do you enjoy teasing me? You're barely wearing anything."

"I'm wearing pajamas," I said hotly, my pulse starting to climb. I was wearing silk blue shorts and a tank top. He pulled away from me in bed and looked up at the ceiling with his hands interlocked behind his head.

"It's time we took a break from each other," he said in a low voice.

"What are you saying?" I asked, unable to believe he was giving up on me that easily. *Was I hearing him correctly?*

"Like I said, we're done, Lacy," he said in a harder tone. "Get dressed. You can leave."

My heart sank, and I got off the bed like it burned me.

In a daze, I pulled on a pair of jeans over my pajamas and a sweater. I couldn't believe he'd do this- his charm and charisma disappearing in seconds. A monster that I wasn't aware of lurking beneath his charming surface.

"Why are you being like this?" I asked, my chest aching. I hoped we'd be something more eventually, and I'd have a pack of my own.

His desire was evident in his gaze, but his frustration was equally apparent. "Lacy, we've been together for months. I care about you, and I want us to be closer."

My brows furrowed. "I care about you too, Jordan, but I need time. I need to feel completely comfortable... before we go any further. Wouldn't you want to wait if you cared about me?"

A tense silence settled over us, broken only by the rain's persistent rhythm. I could feel the weight of Jordan's disappointment pressing against me, a reminder of the unspoken omega expectations that hung between us.

"I can't wait forever, Lacy," Jordan said, his voice tinged with frustration. "If you're not ready to take our relationship to the next level, then maybe we need to reevaluate things. Please leave."

He got up from the bed, and I watched numbly as he grabbed

my purse, walking me to the door. I felt like a throwaway omega. I felt like just a random girlfriend who couldn't fulfill the alpha werewolf's needs.

I was nothing special at all.

He opened the door for me, waiting for me to go. I grabbed my jacket and pulled it on. I didn't have a car, and he wasn't offering to drive me anywhere.

"It's two a.m.," I said, looking at the rain splashing down and the lightning ripping through the sky. Maybe his alpha protective instinct might take over, and he would have a little mercy on me going out this late. If my fathers knew what was happening, they'd rip him to pieces.

"You've wasted enough of my time," he sighed. "An omega should obey her alpha no matter what, and you don't seem to have it in you. It's time to move on. Goodbye, Lacy."

I paused at the door, shocked that our time together meant nothing to him.

"I would only obey someone I respect," I shot back. "Go fuck yourself, Jordan. Good luck finding an omega who'll put up with your sorry ass."

My body shaking with adrenaline, I rushed out of the house, stepping into puddles of water.

He closed the door shut, and I didn't care as I walked to who-knows-where. The hill was slippery as I walked down and away from his stupid house.

I couldn't believe what he said to me.

My clothes stuck to my body from the rain. Tears streamed down my face, mingling with the downpour of the rain. My mom had told me so many times that I was too young to even be thinking about alphas right now, but I never listened. Nineteen was more than old enough to mate a pack. But I didn't see through his charm. He was a typical alpha trying to prime me up for a good knotting.

He didn't care about my comfort or how I felt. He didn't care that I was stuck out here in the middle of nowhere late at night.

I sought shelter under the roof of a dimly lit bar and pulled my phone out with shaking hands. I called my dad, Alex - no response.

My family was definitely sleeping at this time.

I tried calling my cousin Olivia, but there was no response either. I leaned against the wall, looking at the sidewalk drizzled by rain.

I walked into the bar for some warmth. I was numb to the cold, but my body had started shivering while I was outside. My hair was plastered to my face, and I brushed my hair back with my fingers, squeezing the water out of my red hair. I made my way to a bar stool, and the bartender greeted me with a smile. I wasn't in a smiling mood, but I tried my best to look happy as I always did.

"What can I get for you?"

"Just tea," I said.

"We have black tea, green tea, and herbal tea. Which one?"

"Green is fine," I said, not caring as long as it was tea.

"Hot or iced?"

"Hot," I said. I was clearly wet and shivering on this stool. While he walked away to make my tea, I paid more attention to my surroundings.

A band played on the stage, and the music invigorated my soul, reminding me of the days I used to sing for practice in high school. I watched them for a while, lost in my thoughts- thinking about my fresh breakup.

The bartender finally came back with my tea.

"Tough night?" he asked.

I managed a weak smile in return and nodded, wiping my face dry with some napkins he handed me. "Yeah, you could say that."

As I sat there, nursing the warm mug in my hands, my soul was caught by the electrifying sound of the live band of two. One guy was holding an electric guitar, and the other man was singing. The music throbbed with energy, and the lead singer's powerful voice resonated through the room. It was as if the music spoke to his soul, rekindling the fire that Jordan had tried to extinguish.

The bartender leaned in, his voice carrying over the music. "Like what you're hearing?"

I nodded, my eyes fixed on the stage. "Yeah, I love rock music. I used to play in a band myself."

"Really? You play an instrument?"

"The guitar," I replied, a hint of nostalgia in my voice. "But my boyfriend...ex-boyfriend now, I guess. He didn't really support my music. Said it was a waste of time."

His expression turned sympathetic. "Well, it sounds like he didn't appreciate your talent."

The music continued to flow, and my heart began to sync with the rhythm. I downed the last of my drink. "You know what? I'm going to get up there and show him—and myself—that I'm not giving up."

During the break, I worked up the courage to walk to the stage. I didn't want to join them, but I just wanted to sing for a moment.

"Hi," I said. "I love what you're playing."

"Thanks," said the beta male, holding the guitar and wiping his forehead with the back of his tattooed arm.

"I'd like to sing a duet with you guys," I said, my voice shaking a little. I hadn't done this in over a year.

"Of course, you can join," he said.

"Shit, if she got talent, why not?" said the second bandmate. "My name's Ty. The guitarist is Ben."

"Nice to meet you. I'm Lacy," I said, my heart giddy with excitement when they handed me the microphone.

"Which song?" asked Ben.

"Hmm," I said. "How about *Moon's Path* by Gray?"

It was a tear-jerker but powerful song of a pack searching for their lost omega.

"You got it, lady."

I removed my wet jacket and threw it backstage to prepare. My heart fluttered with excitement when Ben strummed the electric guitar. The crowd was silent as they waited for me to start singing. Ty sang the first line for the alpha's part, his voice deep and melodic, transporting me to a different world far away. I joined him during the female's line, elevating my voice - clear and haunting. Inside, I was giddy that I still had it. I could still sing. Our voices intertwined that night, shocking the crowd and causing them to cheer and clap at the end.

I smiled, bowing amidst the clapping.

"Damn, you're good," said Ty, making his way over to me.

"Thanks," I said shyly, handing him the microphone. The lights glowed over us, illuminating the band members' faces.

"What if you joined us? Power band?" said Ty.

"What's the name of your band?" I asked. I was excited at the prospect, but I didn't know them.

"The Beta Guys," said Ty.

"How about Electric Rose?" I suggested, and his lips quirked into a smile.

"I like it," he said.

"Welcome to the team," said Ben, setting down the guitar and staring in wonder at the cheers from the crowd. "You're going to take our band to the next level. I can feel it, Miss Omega. Look at how that crowd adores you already. It's going to be fucking amazing."

.

One

LACY

Five Years Later

I sat cross-legged on my yoga mat as I stared out the window of my home gym.

The view from this window was my favorite. The horizon overlooking the beautiful ocean shore of Howl's Edge Island always calmed me.

For years, my routine consisted of waking up, working out in my gym, and then making a smoothie before I went into the studio to practice with the band.

It was a monotonous routine, but I liked the predictability of it.

Leaving the gym, I walked up the stairs to my kitchen. It was a lot of walking in my dream house after Electric Rose became successful. My home consisted of ten bedrooms and seven bathrooms with an infinity pool, gym, and theater.

I was proud of my accomplishments but also couldn't believe it at the same time.

Setting my freshly-made strawberry smoothie into the refrigerator- I washed the dishes, listening to the news reporter from Howl's Daily.

"This is the seventh omega missing in the string of cases. Authorities are still looking into the cause..."

It was terrible, and I felt bad for the missing omegas. Omegas always went missing, but it was becoming more commonplace.

Most would say my career as a successful singer wasn't safe with all the exposure I was getting, but nothing was going to scare me. After my heartbreak five years ago, I learned never to rely on a potential mate. I wanted to find my way in life without crawling back to my parents. Electric Rose had become a smashing success with the young crowd. They loved it, especially when Ty and I sang together as a duet. It was our trademark and livelihood now.

Drying my hands, I took a few sips of the cool, refreshing smoothie before heading to the shower and getting ready for work. I had taken a week-long vacation, and I was antsy to get back to releasing new songs and singing at our gigs.

My room had bejeweled walls covered from top to bottom, a fur pink rug on the floor, and my bed was covered in matching pillows and pink sheets.

A shelf full of mixed tapes and disks with a radio sitting on top sat in the corner of the room with a poster of my idol, Hayden Gray, above it. He was the most prominent singer of all time on Howl's Edge Island. There weren't many singers, and I was determined to be the first omega singer, which was the best decision I've ever made in my life. I didn't give a damn what anyone thought of me anymore.

My fathers disapproved of my choice for safety reasons and putting myself out there, but my mother was all for it, and I leaned into her support. My older half-brother, Gabe, didn't really care as long as I was happy and making money.

After showering, I picked out a pink skirt that stopped just above my thighs and a white shirt. Fluffing out my long hair, I wore a denim blazer over my shirt.

Finding my purse took forever, but I was finally ready.

My limo was waiting just outside the gate, and I knew my driver, Phil, was most likely annoyed at me right now. I was twenty minutes late to the studio, and I was rushing past the gates to the car. He was patiently holding the door open for me.

"Sorry I'm late as hell," I said, climbing inside the limo.

"That quite alright," he said pleasantly. Then he went to the driver's side. My only view of him was the back of his head, covered in a halo of white hair. "I hope you had a pleasant morning?"

"I did. Did you hear the news about the omegas missing?"

"Yes, it's unfortunate for it to happen in this day and age," he said. "Perhaps, I think it's best you thought about hiring bodyguards?"

"Nope, don't need bodyguards," I said. After my incident with Jordan three years ago, I've counted on only myself.

I've survived on my own, and I'll make it on my own.

~

AT THE STUDIO, Ben and Ty were excited to have me back. They missed me with all the hugs and stories they had to tell. They were pretty much my second family, and I loved being around them, especially when I was feeling lonely.

"You took your sweet time on vacation," said Ben, shaking his head in disappointment. "What did you even do on vacation?"

"I spent time with my family," I said, smiling. I felt like my chosen career had spiraled out of control with fame and constant busy schedules. So it was nice to spend some downtime with my family.

"You have a ton of fan mail there," said Ty, running his hand over his black spiky hair. He wore the same torn black jeans and a plain black shirt with his silver chain. He and Ben were betas, which in the Howl's Edge society meant they didn't have a particular scent associated with them or extra abilities.

Omegas like myself were rare. We were able to produce alpha children if we mated an alpha. Not all the children would end up alpha, but there was a higher probability, and only alphas could shift into werewolf form at will.

Ty led me to the pile of fan mail on the shelf in our dimly lit studio. He pulled out envelopes, flowers, and gifts from my fans.

"Oh, you're right," I said. "That's a lot."

"The mailbox at the building was full," said Ty. "I had to grab them every day for you, but here it is."

I sifted through the envelopes and gifts with a smile. "It's great being back."

"We missed you," said Ty. "Electric Rose isn't the same without you."

"Aww," I said, noticing a small silver box wrapped in a bow. I pulled it open and saw a dead flower petal inside it. On top of it was a tiny scrap of paper, which was hard to read. I made out the words: *Get ready, little Pinkie*

Something about that didn't feel right at all.

"What's wrong?" asked Ty, walking over to my side and peeking at the letter in my hands. When he read the words, he shook his head. "Might be a weirdo. Throw it away, and let's start practicing the song '*Echoes of Tomorrow*.' Full intensity."

"Okay," I said, quickly dumping it in the trash like it was a grenade. I didn't have a good feeling about that gift, and something was ominous about it.

∾

WHEN WE FINISHED RECORDING our new song, I was glad at how amazing it turned out. As I sat in the limo, I couldn't wait to get home and relax before we sang tomorrow in front of a crowd after practicing for hours today. My phone vibrated, and I pulled it out, seeing that I had a missed voicemail.

It had come from an unknown number.

The voice on the other end was deep and disguised, but the words sent chills down my spine.

"Pinkie, why did you throw away the gift, my sweet?"

What. The. Fuck.

Frazzled, I deleted the message and sat still in the limo, breathing hard. The air conditioner hit my legs as I sat there freezing. No one but Ben and Ty were with me in that studio. Only they had seen the note. *Had someone been watching me all day?*

I was too scared to go home now.

"Phil, can you take me to Olivia's, please?"

"Sure," he said.

I dialed Olivia's number, and she answered on the first ring.

"Girl, wassup?" she answered, and I smiled at her familiar voice. She was so down-to-earth, and I needed her at this moment.

"Do you want to go shopping for Alana's baby shower?" I asked. Alana had twins, but now she was having a third baby with her pack. I was happy for her even though it sent little tendrils of envy through me. "It's this Sunday."

"Do I look like I have no life? Just kidding, I don't," said Olivia. "I'll get ready."

"Okay, I'm coming to pick you up."

∾

LATER, we were at the biggest mall on Howl's Edge, which was crowded today. Fall time was always busy as hell. I wore a large hat that I kept in the limo to disguise myself and sunglasses just in case fans mobbed me. I told Olivia everything about the odd gift and the creepy-as-fuck voicemail.

"You need to be careful," said Olivia, while sipping a strawberry icy drink.

"I know," I said. "It's so weird. I don't know how anyone could have seen me throw away the note."

"Do you think it was Ben or Ty playing a prank on you?" she asked.

"They would have called me soon after to laugh about it," I said, shaking my head as I sifted through baby clothes for girls. I held up a pair of overalls. "Do you think this is cute?"

13

"I love the matching purple onesie with it," said Olivia. "Let's get that and maybe a walker."

"I'm fucking scared to go home now," I said as we walked to the baby toys section. The bright colors filled the aisle, and mothers pushing strollers crowded them. I always actively avoided the baby section. It made me sad for some reason, reminding me of the pack life I'd dreamt about before meeting Jordan. I wanted a baby of my own. A pack of my own, but it wasn't time yet.

"Don't be scared," said Olivia. "If you have to, just hire a couple of bodyguards."

"Do you want to sleep over?"

"No," said Olivia quickly, and I rolled my eyes. "I like my own room and bed, sorry cousin. But you can stay at *my* house with your celebrity self."

"I'm not *that* scared," I said, even though I've slept at her house several times. Her mother was my aunt Jade. "But you're right. It could be a prank or something."

"Call the police," said Olivia. She was right about calling the authorities, but I didn't want to make a big deal out of it yet. Nothing *too* crazy had happened so far. Just creepy notes and voicemails.

But when I got home later that night, I knew for sure it wasn't just a prank. I stepped out of the limo, thanking Phil for taking me everywhere today. I walked past the gate towards my front door. My heart stopped at the sight waiting for me.

Dead pink roses were sitting at my doorstep. Someone had managed to get past my high-security gate.

Two

LACY

Looking around in a panic, I slowly picked up the dead bunch of roses and dumped it in the trash. I didn't want my maid coming tomorrow morning to see it and wonder too much about what was happening. She came over once a week to deep clean since I was always busy.

My hands shook as I walked into my house- locking the door behind me.

I ran around the house checking to see if all the windows were closed and all the doors were locked. I felt like I was getting paranoid now.

First, the weird gift, the voicemail, and then the dead flowers? It didn't make any sense, and I started to get frightened. I was used to fan mail and attention, but this one sent a weird chill through my body that I couldn't explain.

After making sure all the doors and windows were secure, I headed into my bedroom and stripped down to my pajamas. When I got ready for bed, I sat on my cozy chair next to my bed to play a little bit of music before I went to bed. I closed my eyes and strummed the guitar as I sang out loud. Every nerve in my body began to relax as I allowed my body to flow with the slow song. I cherished this moment to myself. It didn't happen every night, but only on certain nights when I felt stressed or on edge.

And it was one of those nights.

I slowly set the guitar down, relaxed, and felt my spirit grow stronger. No one was going to scare me. Shutting off all the lights, I lay in bed and closed my eyes. I needed to get enough rest before tomorrow's performance on the beach for the locals. I was stoked about it. It would be the first time we'd done a live performance in a while.

∼

IN THE MIDDLE of the night, I woke up to an odd noise.

I groaned, annoyed, as I opened my eyes in the pitch dark. A loud scuffling sound was coming from outside. I slowly rolled off the bed with memories of yesterday's odd events rushing through my mind. It sounded like someone was jiggling the doorknob from the front door. Anger surged through me, and I grabbed my guitar as a weapon. Running down the stairs, my heart was pounding in my chest.

The noise was for sure coming from the front door.

"Leave!" I screamed at the door.

The sounds stopped, and I heard a low chuckle from the other side. I gripped my guitar high, ready to fling it at his head if he broke in.

I was ready to smash him to bits.

My heart thundered in my ears as I stood there for a long while. When I didn't hear any more noise, I slowly backed away from the door and went to my room.

Locking my room door behind me, I took deep breaths.

I needed to know who this was, and he needed to be arrested. For the rest of the night, I stayed up on my phone looking up the best cameras to install around my house.

∼

THE NEXT DAY, after we finished singing at the concert to the delight of our fans, I was ready to collapse from lack of sleep.

Young fans were reaching out with their hands to the stage, and I high-fived a few of them, smiling. This was always the best part of performances. The look of joy and excitement on everyone's faces invigorated me.

"We love you, Lacy!" screamed a group of teen girls wearing pink and brown, my signature colors. I blew kisses at them and turned to the rest of the Electric Rose group. Ben and Ty were getting their own attention from the fans. Ben gave out autographs using lipstick given to him by a fan.

I grinned at the sight even though a wave of dizziness came over me. I knew I needed sleep, or else I'd collapse.

As I waved and chatted with fans, I felt the hairs on the back of my neck stand up. I couldn't explain it. An eerie, heavy feeling settled over me. A presence watching my every move, or maybe I was just paranoid.

I couldn't shake off the feeling.

I looked around the crowd at every cheering face—nothing out of the ordinary. Then I turned and saw a man standing in the shadows of the building. I couldn't see his face, which was covered by his hoodie.

"Lacy, could you sign this for me?" a fan asked, distracting me.

"Sure," I muttered, turning away from him and quickly signing the fan's flute with a marker. I hastily turned back to see that he had disappeared.

"Alright, thank you, everyone!" said Ty over the microphone, and just like that, it was over after he gave a small speech thanking the crowd for supporting our songs.

"Want to go out for lunch?" Ben asked as we gathered up our instruments.

"I can't, sorry. My wife's cooking tonight," said Ty.

"You look excited," I said, wishing my future husband would

one day be excited at what I made for him. But I couldn't cook to save my life.

"I am. But yeah, we did an amazing job, guys," said Ty, hugging us both. "I'll catch you two later."

With that, we went our separate ways. In the limo, I was glad for the cool air conditioner and the quiet. It had been such a hectic day. I leaned back against the seat, laying a hand on my aching forehead.

"Big day, huh?" said Phil.

"I didn't get enough sleep," I said.

"Why is that?"

"I don't know..." I mumbled, not wanting to divulge what happened. Just thinking about someone on the other side of my front door last night was a nightmare. I didn't want to think about it.

"Take care of yourself," said Phil finally, parking in front of my house.

"I will."

But I wasn't prepared for what I'd find next.

∼

As I WALKED into my home, something on the kitchen counter caught my eye. I wanted to sob with fear when I spotted a little note. Maybe it was my maid leaving me a message, I thought hopefully, but after reading it...I realized it definitely wasn't the case.

Holding the paper in my trembling hands, I read the note again:

You'll be mine soon, Pinkie. And I'll be your breeder. Are you excited for the little alpha babies running around?

My heart was racing out of control at this point.

I dropped the letter back onto the kitchen counter, worried to death that he was lurking in any of the rooms with a knife. He wanted to fucking *breed* me.

Was this another one of those cases where an omega had gone missing? Was I the next target? What the hell did he want with *me*?

I couldn't relax in my home anymore until I called some sort of personal bodyguard service. I really didn't have a choice right now, and I needed them to look around to make sure the creep wasn't hanging around.

But I couldn't stand around the kitchen like a sitting duck.

I ran to the office across from the kitchen and locked the door. I started to look up all the bodyguard services we had on Howl's Edge. I needed the very best. My hands were shaking, and I had to set my phone down for several minutes first. I paced around the office, pondering what to do. I'd avoided hiring bodyguards for so long.

I finally picked my phone back up and dialed.

Three

RYDER

"It's so hot out here," mumbled Adrian as my entire pack watched me aim at the target. The smell of gunpowder surrounded the field of the Elite Protection Club at the gun range.

It was a normal, typical day of bodyguard training.

"Adrian, if I have to hear you complain one more time...I swear to god," I said out loud, trying to aim at the head of the dummy standing on a pole fifty yards away. "I will turn this gun around and shoot you instead."

"Fuck you," mumbled Adrian under his breath.

My pack and I knew that Adrian was nearing the end of his rope at the guard camp. He was the youngest and the most impatient of the group. Even though his family forced him to be here, he wasn't into being a bodyguard. It came naturally to some people, like Ethan, who couldn't wait to shoot the target next - a rifle strapped to his shoulder. He was sitting on the bench along with Lucas and Cooper, the two deltas in my pack.

Ethan, Adrian, and I were alpha wolves.

The other packs were also practicing in the field, and sometimes, I wished I could swap out Adrian with someone who actually liked this job.

I adjusted my goggles and ear protection, feeling a sense of excitement and focus. This was my time to practice and refine my skills. I felt the weight of the pistol in my hand, the cold metal reassuring against my skin. The gun's grip was familiar, molded to fit my hand perfectly. My heart rate slowed as I focused on the target, my surroundings fading away until it was just me and the bullseye.

The round struck the target with a satisfying thud, blowing off the dummy's head.

"Fuck yes," I said. Normally, it would take me two tries, and Ethan would beat me on his first try. But not today. I turned to Ethan with a grin. "Your turn, big guy."

Ethan chuckled, a low rumble in his throat, and his short red beard bobbed.

"You got lucky," said Ethan. "Watch me get closer to the mark there."

But before he could show off his skills and one-up me, our boss, Mark, approached us.

"Uh uh, looks like he has a project for us," said Lucas, who was cleaning his weapon with a rag.

"Goddamn, finally," said Adrian. "We haven't had a client in ages."

Holding my smoking pistol against my side, I watched as Mark approached me with a grim expression. He was a thin beta businessman, always dressed in his everyday navy blue suit. He ran the day-to-day operation of the pack guards.

"Ryder," he greeted, shaking my hand tightly.

"What's going on?" I asked.

"I have a job for you and your pack," he said. "High-profile singer Lacy gave us a call a few minutes ago. She wants the best guards I have available, and I believe your pack will fit the job."

"Shit, I don't know about us being the best," I said.

"She's an omega," said Mark, and I immediately shook my head.

"I think I'll pass on this assignment."

I didn't want to guard a stuck-up little singer and wondered how I'd get out of it. Any other job was better. I'd rather stand guard at an empty lot for the Royal Pack, which was a much better job. At least then, I wouldn't have to suck up to a young omega with her nose in the air.

And an omega was temptation itself.

"You're the best pack, and you know it," said Mark.

"Wait, Lacy?!" asked Adrian with a shocked look.

"Yes, *the* Lacy," said Mark. "I need you guys to head over to her house pronto. She believes someone may have broken in."

"Fuck yes," breathed Adrian, brushing his long black hair away from his eyes. "I'd guard her all day long."

"Then it's decided," said Mark, to my dismay. I didn't have a fucking choice when he made up his mind.

"Listen," said Mark, clapping me on the shoulder. "She was willing to pay any price. You'll be paid handsomely."

"Least that's something," I muttered.

When he left, we gathered our weapons and headed toward the brown armored vehicles. I still wasn't sure about guarding a spoiled brat all day, but the money would speak for itself.

"Are you guys ready?" I asked my pack before we all hopped into the vehicle.

"Of course," said Lucas, ready to defend the omega. He was the stoic delta. Quiet but ready to drop everything if someone's life was in danger.

"I hope you're all prepared," I said to them. I haven't been around an omega for years. They were scarce on Howl's Edge Island. "Omegas are bewitching creatures, and you might all want to do whatever she wants. Remember, you're in charge of her life."

"He's going to suffocate her," said Adrian, shaking his head and Cooper chuckled. They could laugh all they wanted, but an omega's allure was powerful and they wouldn't be laughing anymore once she was in complete control of them.

~

AFTER THIRTY MINUTES OF DRIVING, Cooper stopped in front of the ornate gate of her house.

"Damn, we need to get in," said Cooper. "Can someone call her?"

I pulled my cell phone out and dialed the number that Mark had given us. Lacy answered the phone on the second ring.

"Hello," she greeted uncertainly, as if scared of the other person on the line. I wasn't prepared for the lilt in her tone, breathy and soft. The fear in her voice pulled my heartstrings for a second, but I spoke with business-like authority.

"This is Ryder from Elite Protection Services," I said. "Will you please open the gate for us to come in?"

"Yes, of course!" she said with relief in her voice.

I hung up and watched the gate slowly open at a snail's pace.

"She sounded scared," I said.

"Understandably so," said Cooper, whose hands were impatiently gripping the steering wheel. "Someone tried to break into her home."

I could tell he was itching to search her house and rip apart any degenerate lurking about. When we finally parked in front of her home, Lacy was standing outside, wringing her hands together. There was a sharp intake of breath from the men as we all gazed at her.

Adrian whistled under his breath.

She was a petite omega, shorter than average. Her short, ruffled skirt stopped above her thighs. My heart started pumping faster at the sight of her thighs exposed like that. *Fuck*, I needed to get a handle on myself. I couldn't have this type of reaction my first time meeting her. I pushed my erection down before exiting the vehicle.

I sobered up when I saw the fear and uncertainty in her eyes as we approached her.

Four

LACY

My heart raced when I watched the guards approaching me from the driveway. I could tell instantly who the two deltas were. They towered over the rest of the men at eight feet tall. The three others were alphas, but one looked younger than the rest.

I didn't care, though. I just needed them for protection, and that was it.

The alpha leading them shook my hand first.

The long scar on his forehead and tattoos on his upper arms looked intimidating, but I shook his hand firmly. I was a successful omega who survived for years without an alpha. I had to repeat that over and over in my head not to show any weakness.

"Thank you for coming," I said, smiling politely. He didn't smile back at all, and I wondered what the hell was wrong with him. *Where were his basic manners?* Maybe they raised them tough at the bodyguard service.

"You're welcome," he said. "Name's Ryder. And you're Lacy, correct?"

"Yes," I said. I shook hands with each of the bodyguards as they introduced themselves. Ethan had a short red beard and looked like he was the oldest from the pack. His mannerism was gentlemanly, kissing my hand during our introduction.

"I'm Adrian," said the youngest one of the group, his black hair messy around his shoulders. "I may be the youngest, but I'm not lacking. You can trust me with your life."

I laughed at his frankness.

"I'm trusting you," I said.

Adrian winked, and their alpha leader, Ryder, rolled his eyes. I already liked Adrian. He had that type of personality I got along with. He was easygoing and didn't take himself too seriously.

"Enough flirting," said Ryder gruffly. "Take us through what happened. What did you see or hear?"

I took a deep breath, remembering all the crazy events that happened in the past two days. I told him everything I could remember, even the creepy voicemail.

"So now I'm scared to sleep in my house because he could be in any of the rooms," I said.

Saying it out loud sounded so ridiculous I was embarrassed.

"The pack will do a check of your home," said Ryder without blinking an eye. "Guys, check every room and cranny. We need to make sure the vagrant isn't still lurking about."

I led them inside the house and watched them all go in different directions. The delta named Cooper checked the outside, and Lucas went upstairs. Adrian and Ethan headed downstairs to check out the basement and theater.

"I feel much safer already," I said to Ryder, who stood with me in the kitchen as he stared at the note on the counter without touching it.

"Do you know who could have written this note?" he asked, taking several pictures of it and placing it in a bag while wearing gloves.

"Not really," I said. "This never happened before."

"With the string of omega cases on the news- anything is possible," he said, pocketing the note. "First thing is we need to install cameras in your home. I'm surprised you didn't install any. A high-profile singer such as yourself needs it."

"Umm, yeah," I said. "I didn't have time to look into that. But yes, you're right."

"For now, we will install one in your living room. Next, I'll need to know your schedule," he said, taking out a notepad and pen. I was surprised by the intensity and seriousness of this whole thing. I was usually very flippant about my safety and couldn't care less. But these incidents did strike fear in me.

"I go to the studio around nine in the morning," I said.

"We'll meet you here tomorrow and escort you to the studio," he said. "May I see your phone, please?"

"For?"

"The voicemail," he said.

"But I deleted it."

"There are ways to recover it," he said, holding his hand out with contained patience. I could tell he was getting irritated with me, but I didn't care. It was my personal belonging. I unlocked my phone and handed it to him, worried about what he'd find. "What's this?"

"What?" I asked, my heart pounding as I peered at the phone. He somehow managed to pull up an old deleted video of some porn I watched a few days ago. I gritted my teeth with annoyance. "That's totally unnecessary."

"I'm just going through your deleted files," he said. His lips twitched, and I knew he thought it was amusing to find that on my phone. I was mortified. I thought I'd gotten rid of it forever and even deleted it twice, but he managed to pull it up from the recesses of my phone. "There. Is this it?"

He played the voicemail on the speaker. The eerie masked voice playing in the kitchen felt like a violation. It made me feel sick.

"That's the one," I said.

"I'll forward it to myself," he said. Then he handed my phone back. "I added my phone number in your contacts so you'll know right away who's calling."

"Oh, okay, thanks," I said. I was usually so disorganized and clumsy about these things. He was precise in his job and organized on a level I'd never been before.

The guards returned to the kitchen, standing around the granite top I was leaning on. Being surrounded by all these males after years of being alone was odd. My middle clenched unwillingly. I took a couple of deep breaths to calm down. As an omega, it was tough inhaling the alphas' scents. Their scent was made to arouse an omega and to make her submit underneath him, legs spread.

It was in our biology. It's why I had to take heat suppressants daily.

"Everything looks good," said Ethan, rubbing his beard. "Hopefully, Ryder wasn't giving you a hard time, my darling."

"Nope," I said with a smile. The only serious person here was Ryder, who hadn't cracked a smile the entire time except when he discovered the offending video on my phone. Maybe he took delight in my discomfort.

"Alright then, we'll see you tomorrow," said Ryder. "I advise you not to leave your home under any circumstances unless one of us is around you. Call me if anything happens between now and tomorrow."

"Sounds peachy," I said.

He looked pained by my choice of words, and I held back my laughter. He was *way* too serious. But I didn't take life too seriously myself, so maybe he was right. Adrian was staring at me the entire time, and my body heated under his gaze. I looked at him to tell him to back off, but when we made eye contact, he gave me a crooked smile, which made my stomach flip.

"See you later," said Adrian, the last one standing with me at the door. He was taking his sweet time to leave.

"You better not flirt with me," I said. "Everything is staying as professional as possible."

He cocked his head to one side, giving me the most smoldering look he could muster, making me laugh. He was going to be trouble.

"You sure?"

"Get out of here," I said, ready to slam the door in his face. "I don't know how I'm going to work with you."

"Soon, you'll wonder how you ever survived without me," he said. "No, I'm kidding. I'll do my best- just hard to concentrate with how pretty you are."

"Bye, Adrian," I said finally, and he left.

I closed the door, breathing hard.

I felt much better in my home after they searched it, but I was also nervous about what the coming days would hold. Pressing a hand between my legs, I was horny as hell around these bodyguards. Their scents and presence had driven my hormones crazy as an omega. I quickly went to the couch and pulled my phone out with one hand cupping my pussy underneath my skirt.

Laying on the couch, I pulled up a hot video of two alphas massaging a naked omega on a white table. Her flushed skin and moans filled the screen as I watched an alpha slowly work his finger into her shiny oiled pussy. His thick finger spread her wide, made me breathe harder. I imagined his finger spreading my pussy. The second alpha was rubbing her clit and belly. Soon, they would knot her, just warming her up.

I stuffed my hand inside my panties and rubbed myself in circles with two fingers as I watched. I was getting too hot. I removed my top and skirt, sitting in only my pink bra and panties. I watched the alpha pumping his dick in his other hand, inches from her pussy, while the second one already had his dick deep in her mouth.

I rubbed faster and faster as he speared her pussy with his cock.

Her buttocks clenched as he pressed his entire length into her. I hesitantly tried to press a finger inside of me, but I was scared when I felt my hymen. Instead, I rubbed my clit as I watched him fuck her on the table while she swallowed the cum of the other alpha. *Moons, I wish that was me.*

I closed my eyes and leaned against the couch, imagining it was one of my bodyguards rubbing my clit. I basked in the guilty pleasure until I cried out with my orgasm.

"Oh, Ryder," I moaned out loud as I lay slumped on the couch with aftershocks going through my body. It took a while to regain my breathing as I tried to collect myself. Opening my eyes, I noticed something dark and round on the corner of the ceiling.

Oh, my fucking moons...

The camera.

I completely forgot that Ryder had one of his men install a camera there. Scrambling off the couch, I grabbed my clothes and ran upstairs to my room. *How could I be so stupid?!* They'd just told me a camera was installed, and the first thing I did was freaking masturbate right there in the open. I frantically wondered how I could remove the footage. I sat on my bed mortified, hoping against hope none of them saw or cared to watch it.

This is exactly why I hated cameras.

I was dying to call Olivia so she could make me feel better about it, but it was too fucking embarrassing. I couldn't do that. The only thing I could hope for was that they didn't care enough to watch anything from today. *Did they even have access to it outside my home?* I had no idea how any of it worked, but my face was burning that night as I tried to sleep.

Five

RYDER

An hour after we returned from Lacy's place, I slammed the door shut to my room.

It had been an interesting day being around an omega after not being around one for many years. If I hung around her any longer, her presence alone would've driven me into a rut. She needed to put on more scent blockers, and I planned to tell her that tomorrow if she was going to be around us for too long. Then I remembered that I didn't smell any scent on her. I couldn't pinpoint her scent, and an omega's scent is usually obvious to an alpha. It was confusing to me, so maybe she put on a ton of scent blockers already.

But her presence alone still affected me.

I stripped off my boots and clothes, only wearing boxers. The guard center had separate rooms for all the bodyguards and free food, which was nice. After eating dinner with my pack, I blasted the air conditioner and flopped onto the bed. It felt good to strip down and let loose finally. My cock was aching ever since leaving the omega - a natural response to her pheromones. I started going through the camera footage of her house on my phone. She was careless and annoying, but I enjoyed being around her feminine beauty and... *What the fuck?*

I pulled up the video feed on my phone to check on her house, but I could see her on the couch with her legs spread.

Fuck, I knew I shouldn't be watching this, but I couldn't help myself.

I gripped my cock, watching her on the screen, pleasuring herself. She was even more beautiful on the screen. I turned up the volume, and the sound of her moans filled the room. I pumped my cock frantically as I watched her fingering herself underneath her little panties.

My breathing was strained as I watched. She winced for a second before resuming to rub herself.

Was she trying to put a finger inside? She was probably a virgin. My cock hardened and grew even more at that. She had never let an alpha near enough to knot her.

I pumped faster and faster, watching her legs tremble as she watched whatever porn was on her phone. I was curious what she was watching this time. Then she screamed out my name.

"Fuck," I growled, feeling my seed spill all over my wrist. She had called out *my* name.

I couldn't believe it.

I watched her face turn pink with realization upon seeing the camera and then scurrying away. Poor girl. I did warn her about the camera, but again, she was careless, making me want to protect her even more.

Playing the video back, I smiled while listening to her moan and scream out my name again. I was going to listen to this on repeat all night, and I knew my arm was going to be fucking sore. Lacy was a beautiful omega, and to have her scream out my name was a pleasure I couldn't explain. Maybe it was some kind of alpha ego. I couldn't fucking explain it. But she needed to know that all the porn she watched was fake.

Sex was dirty, sweaty, and full of liquids. Not staged and perfect like what she was watching.

Six

LACY

I didn't want to go outside the next morning to greet my bodyguards.

Still embarrassed from last night, I stood in front of the door for a couple of minutes while they waited outside for me. My heart was pounding hard, and I couldn't seem to get over it. I wanted to die after masturbating in front of a camera last night.

I was saving my body for the right alpha and his pack- and until that time came, I never wanted to be exposed like that to anyone.

Opening the door, I saw all five of them standing there waiting for me. My cheeks flushed pink as if I was standing naked before them. Ryder had an odd glimmer in his eye. No, I needed to stop being paranoid. They had no reason to watch the cameras under any circumstances. And I told myself they couldn't watch the feed outside my home.

"Good morning, ma'am," said Adrian, saluting me.

"Morning," I said dryly. "You can just call me Lacy."

"Awesome, so we're on a first-name basis now," said Adrian. I was most nervous about seeing Ryder. The scar on his face shone more in the bright sunlight. He didn't have any facial hair, so his rough features stood out even more. My heart raced, and I didn't realize how sweaty my palms were until I wiped my hands on my bright blue skinny jeans.

"Hello, Lacy," he said. His drawling voice sent butterflies to my stomach, which I didn't expect. Maybe it was the combination of being mortally embarrassed and him likely seeing what happened in my living room last night. Or maybe he hadn't seen the video. I would never know. "We should get going."

"You guys can follow behind me. I'm having my driver take me with the limo," I said.

"Then we're all coming with you," said Ryder, and the rest of the pack nodded. "Everywhere you go, we're hired to be with you. We take no chances."

"Oh, umm," I said, seeing there was no way out of this. I was starting to regret hiring bodyguards. If they got too close and smelled my true scent, they'd laugh. They were going to follow me no matter what. "Yeah, that's fine, I guess."

I walked to the limo, holding my little black clutch with shaking hands.

The deltas immediately flanked me on both sides, and the alphas walked in front and behind me. A sense of power and accomplishment flowed through me at the bodyguards following me. Now, I would be able to go through large crowds easily without Ben and Ty having to suffer for me.

Phil opened the door for us, bug-eyed at the five muscular men surrounding me.

"Morning Phil," I said. "Meet my personal bodyguards. This is Ryder, the pack alpha. This is Ethan, Cooper, Lucas, and Adrian."

"Nice to meet you all," nodded Phil.

"Likewise," said Ryder gruffly.

They all shook hands, introducing themselves to each other as I crawled into the limo. I sat to the far right, pushing myself against the wall so we could all have enough space for ourselves. I was a trembling mess just by shaking Ryder's hand. I needed as much space from them as possible.

33

Adrian came in after me, sitting right next to me. The rest of the bodyguards crowded inside, and the limo never felt so small before. Once everyone was inside and the door was shut, I started feeling heady with arousal as I took in all their different scents. Adrian's powerful thighs touching mine sent my mind into a spiral of dirty desires.

I wanted to sit on his lap and grind on him.

Sometimes, I felt like I had sexually repressed myself on purpose because of my mother's reputation on Howl's Edge. When the kids started to make fun of me in school about my mom being the alpha king's whore, I cried at home until she explained her version of the story. My mother, Vanessa, was the toughest omega I knew, and I would always admire my mother no matter what the kids said.

But that made me try even harder not to be like her.

I didn't want to have a child I didn't plan for or get myself into trouble taking an alpha that wasn't mine. My half-brother Gabe didn't care what anyone thought of our mom. He was an extrovert and thrived on the attention of the Royal Pack since King Armon was his father.

The Royal Pack didn't pay attention to me as much as they did my precious brother, but I was glad. I didn't need attention from them.

"Hope you slept well last night?" asked Adrian, turning to me. I looked around at all the men nervously. Ryder's lips twitched, and I panicked inside, wondering if he'd been watching the cameras.

"I did, thank you," I said, trying to focus my gaze elsewhere. But the limo was full, and everywhere I turned, I locked eyes with one of them.

"After we left your residence, I presume you felt much safer?" asked Ryder with a lilt in his tone that only I noticed.

It made my heart beat faster. *He knew.*

"Yes," I said, clearing my throat loudly to block out any

awkwardness in my answer. I stared boldly at him to show that he didn't intimidate me in the slightest. *I* was his employer.

He smiled, and I quickly turned away.

"We'll have to check the cameras later to see if Lacy's stalker returns," said Ethan gruffly.

"No, it's okay," I squeaked in a panic. Ryder's smile widened, and that's when I knew for sure that he watched it. My pussy clenched painfully, and my head spun.

"You're right, Ethan," said Ryder. "But it'll be best if I check it first. If I see anything, I'll send it to you because god knows that I have enough to analyze."

When he spoke the last line, he was looking directly at me. My face couldn't get any more hotter than it already was. The limo was stuffy and full of males. I had to get out of here, but there was another ten more minutes before we arrived at the studio.

Even though the air conditioner was on, I tried to fan myself with my hands.

"Are you okay there, Miss Lacy?" asked Cooper, the delta with blue eyes and long locks of blond hair. Even though he towered above everyone, his hands were slim, and his suit immaculate.

"Doesn't it feel a little stuffy in here?" I asked.

"Give her some space, Adrian," ordered Ryder in a sharp voice. "This omega is in distress."

"A wet towel to her forehead might help," said Ethan worriedly.

"No, it's okay. It's not Adrian," I protested, taking deep breaths, but that only made me more drunk off their male scents.

Adrian scooted over to give me room and turned up the air conditioner so it was blasting towards me. Ryder poured water onto a towel from a water bottle and knelt before me, pressing it to my forehead. His closeness made me nearly hyperventilate. He looked concerned as he pressed the wet towel to my forehead. I felt the cool air on my face and took a few deep breaths. Their scents were not as strong anymore, and I started feeling more clear-headed.

"I'm okay now," I said, wrapping my fingers around his forearm to pull him away.

The muscles on his arm bunched, and my heart palpitated audibly in my chest.

I pressed my thighs close together so he didn't notice my scent. Every morning, I slathered on a bunch of scent blocker lotion because I was embarrassed by the scent that emerged from me during puberty. My scent was ginger-like, which wasn't pleasant like all the other omegas. I wished my omega scent was flowers or candy- anything but ginger. It was a sweet-smelling ginger.

But it was still *ginger*.

"I don't think so," he said in a low voice so only I could hear him. I was breathing hard, trying not to perfume. My scent blocker cream was the most powerful one I could find in the stores. It felt like it was only me and him in this space. The close-ness of his body and the deep baritone of his voice was causing havoc on my body.

I couldn't think straight.

"I'm okay, I swear," I said. Ryder pressed his hand over my left breast, and I jumped.

"I need to make sure your heartbeat is normal," he said calmly. His hand was causing my heart to race even faster. "You're not used to being around so many males, huh?"

"No," I whispered.

He removed his hand from my breast, and I could breathe easier again.

"Take deep breaths, omega," he said. His eyes glowed, having discovered that I was a virgin.

"I'm sorry, I don't know why this is happening," I said.

"Don't be sorry," he said. "It's not something you can control. Some omegas are more sensitive to alphas than others."

"I think I feel better now, though," I said, trying to reassure him.

He slowly removed the wet towel from my forehead, and Adrian handed me some napkins to wipe off the cool moisture. Ryder returned to his seat directly across from me, watching me closely.

During the rest of the ride, I leaned back against my chair and closed my eyes, trying to regulate my breathing. I never felt like this around my ex-boyfriend, not even remotely, even though he was an alpha. My feelings were much more heightened around these males. I don't know if it was because of Adrian and Cooper's devilishly handsome looks and Ryder's gruffness. My ex wasn't bad-looking, but maybe our scents just didn't align. It was a possible factor in why a mating wouldn't work out.

I grew worried about my future now.

I breathed in the air conditioner as Phil parked the limo, unaware of what was occurring in the back of his limo. All the alphas could be knotting me in the back, and he wouldn't even know.

"Where are you guys going to go while I practice?" I asked.

"Half of us will be with you inside," said Ryder.

"Listen, I'm not in any danger inside the studio," I said. "Ben and Ty are in there, so it'll be fine."

"Who the hell are Ben and Ty?" asked Ryder.

"Haven't you heard of the Electric Rose?" asked Adrian, rolling his eyes at his pack leader's cluelessness. "They're her bandmates. I can't wait to meet them."

Seven

RYDER

I didn't care if Ben and Ty were her fucking bandmates or her brothers. I had to ensure our omega was safe and intact everywhere she went. We were paid to do one job, and I was going to do it well.

We were the best security on Howl's Edge.

As I watched her singing to Ty's guitar playing, I couldn't help but wonder why Lacy freaked out in the limo like that. She had to be a virgin. That was the only explanation for her reaction being in close proximity to us. When I pressed the towel onto her forehead, I smelled her scent for a brief moment before she shut her legs tight.

It was a sweet scent with a hint of bitterness to it. I couldn't place it.

But I knew I didn't get enough of it.

My dick was hard as fuck while I watched her shaking her hair wildly as she sang in the dark little studio. I couldn't go near her like that again, or else our jobs would be over. I needed to be more careful. We were only here to guard her, not knot her and mark her forever as ours. The thought was appealing as I watched the gap between her thighs separate as she sang. I wanted to bend her over the table and pull down her clothes to expose her little panties.

Then I'd spank her for not installing the cameras in her house. *Fuck, my dick was stone now.* I would then make her play with her pussy while I spanked her, then I'd pound my cock into her pink little pussy until she screamed my name to stop.

I was snapped out of my trance when I saw her looking at me. I smiled at her calmly, like I wasn't thinking such dirty thoughts about her, and she smiled back at me like an angel. *Damn, I needed fresh air.*

"Keep an eye on her," I told Cooper and Adrian. They were standing at the back entrance.

"You got it," said Adrian, giving me a salute. It was hard to be angry at Adrian even though he was the laziest guy in my pack. He never took anything personally, and he was quick-witted, which we needed on our team. The deltas in my pack were the most serious guys I've ever met on the island. They took their job seriously at the bodyguard camp before we formed into a pack. We all naturally gravitated towards each other, forming a lifelong pack, as do most packs on Howl's Edge.

I walked outside the studio, and the bright sun flashed in my face. I pulled my sunglasses down and walked around the perimeter of the building, nearly crashing into Ethan and Lucas. Lucas's eyes were narrowed like he'd seen something.

"What's going on Lucas?" I asked.

"We saw some dude wearing a gray sweatshirt creeping around the trees there," said Lucas, pointing to a general area behind the studio. The back of it was covered in trees, away from the main road.

"Did you see his face?" I asked. This could be her stalker.

"No, but I took a picture just as he slunk away," Ethan pitched in, pulling out his camera. I studied the still image of the guy. He wore a black baseball hat without a strand of his hair sticking out, dirty sneakers, and an oversized gray sweater.

"Prime suspect," I said. "There's no reason for him to be hanging around here. Did he see you guys?"

"That's when he ran away," said Lucas. "He didn't expect us to come around to the back."

"Then this isn't some innocent mega-fan of hers," I said, coming to the realization that she could be in more danger than I thought. It wasn't a spoiled girl crying wolf. But I didn't want to jump to conclusions either. "We'll look for clues later, and I'll study the image more closely."

"Just like you studied the camera feed from last night?" asked Ethan with a wide smile.

"Fuck, you saw it too?" I asked.

"Damn right, I want to make sure she's safe," said Ethan. "She might have a thing for you."

"Wait, what?" asked Lucas, completely lost about what we were discussing.

"It's nothing," I said quickly.

I didn't want the omega to be embarrassed.

Growing up, I've been around alphas who talked crudely of omegas, in which I've participated on a few occasions. It was guy talk, but for some reason, I felt slightly overprotective of Lacy. She didn't deserve it.

"What do you mean 'nothing'? It was the hottest damn thing," grunted Ethan, remembering. I also remembered how her thighs shook as she came. "Poor omega. She needs a pack of her own."

"Damn, she was touching herself?" asked Lucas.

I heard a throat clearing behind me, and I spun around, my hand gripping the handle of my pistol. Oh, it was only Adrian and Cooper. But Lacy was standing in the middle of them, her face bright red like her hair.

Fuck my life.

Did she hear us discussing her masturbation session from last night?

Eight

LACY

I was mortified.

They were talking about the footage on camera from my living room last night. That was the only thing Lucas could be talking about when he asked Ryder if I was touching myself. They *had* to be talking about me.

I could barely breathe. Before walking into them, I was so hyped and excited about the song I practiced earlier and enjoyed the eye fucking from Ryder. Oh yes, I noticed the looks and stares he gave me the entire time. I wasn't born yesterday, even though I was a virgin.

But I had to be the boss omega. I needed to show them I wasn't fazed at all, so I didn't react to Lucas's statement.

"I'm in the mood for some ice cream," I told them. Lucas nodded quickly as if he was guilty.

"You sure you don't want to go home?" asked Ryder. He looked at me with a studying gaze like he wanted to dominate and swallow me whole. Like he couldn't believe I just asked to go out for ice cream.

Good.

"I'm very sure," I said firmly, spinning around on my heels

and walking to the limo. "Today was a great fucking day at work, and I need something for my throat."

"Aren't warm liquids better?" asked Adrian, out of breath as he came up beside me.

"Well, I'm in the mood for ice cream," I said haughtily. He looked taken aback as he opened the door for me before Phil could walk around the limo. "Phil, please take me to *Celestia's Confections.*"

"Of course," he said, staring daggers at Adrian. Phil took pride in his work and wanted to be the one who held the door open for me, so he stood there awkwardly with his arms hanging at his sides.

"Thanks," I said, going inside and sitting all the way in the corner like before. Adrian naturally sat next to me, but he looked at me with concern.

"Is there something wrong, Lacy?"

"No, nothing," I said quickly as I watched Ryder, Ethan, Cooper, and Lucas come in after us. They didn't need to hear how rattled I was that they'd watched me last night. Ryder had probably jerked off to my video. *Whatever*. I didn't care anymore at this point since it was too late.

When they closed the door, I didn't look at any of them-occupying myself with my phone instead and trying to play a game I hadn't played in a while. The limo was quiet, besides the light hum of the air conditioner. I could hear the men breathing all around me, and I felt like all of their gazes were on me.

"Lacy," said Ryder.

"Yes?" I said, swallowing nervously and looking up. *Act tough. Be the tough omega boss you are.*

"We saw some suspicious activity outside your studio," he said. My heart started palpitating with worry now. "A man was sneaking around, trying to look through the studio windows, but when he saw us- he ran."

"Oh wow," I said, not knowing what else to say. There was an actual creep after me, and he wasn't going away. "So there *is* someone after me. What the hell could he want?"

"He could be a fan who took it to another level," said Lucas. It was the first time Lucas talked directly to me, and I was surprised as I looked at him next. He had brown hair in a buzz cut and one silver earring hanging from his left ear. He was the bigger delta of the two and huskier.

"Ugh, I'm legit freaked out now," I said, hugging myself from the cold air. Adrian gave me some space, and I was grateful. His scent, along with all the others, could send me into a panic again.

"Don't be," said Ryder. "We'll find him, and he'll go to prison for harassing you."

"Prison is not a great place at all," laughed Ethan. "He'll regret it."

It was true. The prison on Howl's Edge Island was no joking matter. They placed prisoners in wet dungeons with no real beds or food. I wouldn't care if the stalker was jailed. He broke into my house, and now he was sneaking around my workplace. It was disturbing.

The bodyguards could shoot him on sight for all I cared.

~

THE STRAWBERRY MIXED with chocolate ice cream tasted cool on my tongue as I sat on one of the tables outside the shop. The tables had cute blue umbrellas, shading customers from the sun as they ate. My bodyguards stood around me, adjusting their sunglasses and clearing their throats constantly as they waited for me to finish. I knew Ryder was low-key annoyed as fuck at me. He deserved it if he watched the video from last night and bragged about it to everyone.

"I'd like to buy an ice cream cone," said Adrian.

"If you must," grunted Ryder, his jaw tightening as he adjusted his sunglasses. The customers kept looking at our table and the weird arrangement of all five men standing around me with guns in their holsters.

I licked my ice cream, staring at the sunset, thinking about everything. I felt much safer than I had in days ever since hiring the bodyguards, so it wasn't a mistake. The only drawback was the camera they installed at the house, which I hated.

Adrian plopped into the chair beside me, licking the lemon gelato ice cream he ordered.

"Damn, this tastes so good," he said, licking it with his eyes rolled back in pleasure. His excitement at the amazing organic taste of the ice cream already put me in a better mood.

"Have you ever had Celestia's ice cream before?" I asked, giggling, as I crunched the sweet strawberry chunk.

"Mhm, no," he said, taking another giant lick. I couldn't help but notice the wideness of his tongue, and my stomach clenched with arousal. I quickly looked at my dripping ice cream and licked it off.

Cooper had also bought ice cream and sat on my other side. His long blond hair got stuck in the ice cream, and Adrian laughed as he cursed up a storm, flinging his sticky hair behind his shoulders.

"Yeah, this shit's good," said Cooper, relaxing back in his chair.

"She didn't pay us to eat ice cream," growled Ryder, who was clearly unhappy with this arrangement. Ethan and Lucas were like robots, constantly on the lookout, so he didn't need to worry about them.

"It's okay," I said in a calming tone. I enjoyed having the two men eat ice cream with me, and it felt different than eating alone. "The stalker would never show up here. He knows you guys are with me now. Plus, I feel less alone."

"Aw," said Adrian, rubbing my arm in affection. My face grew warm at the contact, and noticing my face flush, he removed his hand.

At that moment, I heard my phone ding with a text message.

Upon seeing the unknown number, I unlocked my phone on the table with apprehension.

It said:

Enjoy the ice cream while it lasts. Soon, I'll lick you up when you're mine, little pinkie.

I gasped- ignoring the dripping ice cream in my hand.

"What's going on?" asked Ryder, quickly snatching up my phone.

"Hey!" I shouted as his eyes skimmed the text message.

"It's him," he said. At his words, Adrian and Cooper jumped off their chairs, flinging their ice creams into the trash and standing around me like a fortress protecting me from the enemy. Ryder handed my phone back to me and pulled his gun out instead. "We need to get her back to the car. Now."

I looked around frantically, my heart beating fast as they herded me back to the limo. A guard covered every opening around me as they tightened the circle around me. Their muscular planes pressed against my body as we slowly walked while Ryder scoped out the area.

"He's here if he knows she's eating ice cream," Ethan told Ryder.

"I don't see the guy with the gray sweater," said Ryder. "He knows what he's doing, and I'm not happy about it."

Once in the limo, I was relieved to be out of sight of the stalker. I didn't even care about how close Adrian was sitting to me. I looked at the text message again, and chills went up my spine.

He had been watching me eat ice cream.

I was starting to get annoyed and frustrated as I finished the rest of my ice cream. But I jumped when my phone started to ring. All the men sat on the edge of their seats in alarm.

"Oh, it's just my nephew," I said out loud, looking at the name on the screen and feeling silly. Manfred was my nephew- the son of Princess Lyra. "Hey, Manny."

"Hey, what's up?" he said in his usually bored drawling voice.

To me, he was the jokester and never took life seriously. We were close in age, and he was even older than me, so we were more like best friends. We weren't exactly blood-related, but my brother was his blood uncle.

"Nothing," I said, trying to breathe evenly.

"You sound like something frightened you," he said. "Anyways, I have something to tell you. You won't believe it."

"Okay, what is it?" I asked, rolling my eyes.

"My family finally agreed to host a haunted house event," he said excitedly. "I want you to come, and you can bring Olivia too."

"Ooh, that's exciting," I said, smiling but also partly relieved it wasn't my stalker calling. "When do you want us there?"

"How about this Sunday?"

"Oh no, that's Alana's baby shower."

"Monday night then," he said.

"I have work."

"Please."

"Fine, I'll try," I said, sighing. "It better be worth it."

"Oh, it will. This year's scare event is going to be so fucking awesome. Can't wait to see you."

"Alright, bye, Manny."

"Bye-bye."

As I hung up, I noticed Ryder staring at me with a hard expression on his face.

"I don't know how I feel about you going to that," said Ryder.

"Hey, you can't control what I can and cannot do," I said.

"That's true, but this is for security purposes," he said. "Anything could happen."

"Listen, let's just see what happens over the next few days," I said, biting my lower lip. Ryder had a point- but I couldn't live in fear just because a crazy stalker was after me. I still had to support my nephew and be there for him.

Nine

LACY

T onight was going to be a self-care night. Today's events had rattled me too much. I was tired of it, so I sat in my bubbly bathtub, enjoying the peace. Grabbing my red waterproof vibrator, I slowly rubbed it over my thighs as I leaned back in the tub.

Once again, being around the pack for hours had turned me on a lot, and I needed relief. I've never masturbated for two days in a row, and I wondered what was happening to me. I justified it by the stressful day I went through. I leaned back in the tub, enjoying the bubbles that rose to my chin. The air was foggy with the hot bath, and the scent of my body wash mixed with my ginger scent filled the air.

Even though I used the strongest body wash, it wasn't enough to erase my natural smell. My skin tingled with the vibrating toy between my thighs, and my body grew warmer with arousal. I pressed the toy against my pussy, pressing it's rubber ear inside my pussy. It didn't go all the way in, but just enough so I could feel something there. The toy vibrated under the water against my clitoris, and my breathing came out in harsh gasps the closer I got to my orgasm. I thought about all the bodyguards and how close their bodies were to mine in the limo. I thought about Ryder watching me masturbate, and my face heated, but my pussy clenched.

I shivered around the toy as I came thinking about him.

Damn.

I came down slowly from my high, spent and trembling as I lay in the tub, letting my toy drop to the bottom. My pussy clenched from the aftershocks, and I wished I had an alpha's knot to relieve me. Staying a virgin was much harder now that I was constantly around alphas and deltas. And they were hot as hell on top of that. After Jordan, I never dated anyone but instead focused on my dream of singing. But now...I was starting to re-think my entire life.

Suddenly, I heard the sound of a crash coming from downstairs.

I stilled in the water, listening intently. Maybe an animal knocked over my flower vase, even though I had no pets. A squirrel must have gotten in. But when I heard footsteps shuffling around downstairs, my heart stopped. Heart pounding hard, I slowly stood up from the bathtub, stark naked and trying not to make a noise. I grabbed my towel, wrapping it around my chest. I needed to barricade myself in my room and get to my phone.

Heart-racing, I ran from the bathroom and went into my room. I slammed my bedroom door shut and locked it with pruney fingers. The footsteps started running up the stairs after figuring out where I was.

Fuck.

Breathing hard through my nose, I swiped my phone from my bed with shaking hands. I tried dialing Ryder's number, but my fingers were wet. Rubbing my hands on my towel, I tried again.

Harsh knocking sounded at the door, and I instantly dropped my phone, which slipped from my wet hands.

"Get out of my house!" I screamed. Silence on the other side.

I watched in horror as the person tried jiggling the doorknob. *Oh, hell no.* Picking up my phone from the floor, I ran to the walk-in closet and shut the door. I sat in front of the door, leaning my back against it as I tried to dial Ryder's number again. My vision was blurry from my panic, and my hands wouldn't stop shaking as I held the phone to my ear.

Ryder answered on the first ring.

"Yes?"

"There's someone in my house," I whispered shakily, trying to speak above the noise of the banging at the door. "I'm in my bedroom, and he's trying to get in. Please come."

"I'm already halfway to your house," he said in a firm voice. "Get inside your closet."

"Okay, I am," I said.

"Wrap a bunch of clothes around your arm in case they come at you with a knife," he ordered.

I scrambled around my closet, pulling glittery dresses off the racks in my panic. I tried to wrap them around my arms, but then I heard the banging at the door get even louder. I kept dropping the clothes and picking them up again.

Louder rattling as he fiddled with the doorknob. I tried to wrap the clothes around my arms as best I could. I scrambled to pick up the phone.

"Okay, I did it," I said as the glitter scratched my arms.

"Good girl. It's in case you have to lift your arm to block off a knife attack," he said.

"Okay," I whispered.

"Stay on the line with me, Lacy. Don't hang up," he said, and I heard him bark commands to his pack while I stayed on the line with him. I sat huddled in the closet for what seemed like an eternity. I closed my eyes, listening to the banging and the shaking of the doorknob.

Emotions ran through me, especially rage. *Who the hell did he think he was?*

"Leave!" I screamed again, clutching the phone tight in my hands. "You jackass!"

"Don't antagonize him. I'm almost there."

Just then, I heard my bedroom door crash open.

My heart raced through the roof as I sat there, trying to breathe quietly. I was a dead omega tonight.

That was all there was to it.

I envisioned my parents crying over my stabbed body and my brother losing his mind with grief. Tears flowed down my cheeks. I waited for the killer to burst into the closet, and I braced myself, pressing my back against the door.

I sat up straighter, trying to hear what was going on. Then I heard my front door slam open and footsteps running upstairs.

"Lacy," shouted Ryder's voice.

Sighing hugely in relief, I unwrapped the clothes from my arms and stood up on shaky legs. I was scared to open the closet door if the stalker was still lurking there. So I stood there trembling until Ryder opened the door. At the sight of his face, tears of relief ran down my face.

I threw myself at him, hugging him around the waist.

He pressed his nose to my neck and purred deeply into me. Low rumbles of his purr vibrated through my body, calming every nerve inside me.

"Where is he?" I said in a low voice, still unable to let go of Ryder. I wanted to rub my face in his chest and drink in his calming presence.

"We didn't see anyone," he said, lifting his face from my neck, and the purring stopped.

"That means he's still out there," I said, panicking. "He was just here! I swear."

"I believe you, Lacy. I heard everything on the phone. My pack is looking all over and doing a thorough search of your home," said Ryder. "As of right now, it's unsafe for you to continue to live here."

"Wait, what do you mean?"

"You can come with us to a secure location," he said.

My pulse was racing, and I tried to think of any way to stay. I needed to be in my home for comfort and anything else I needed. I hated sleeping elsewhere.

"How about- if you and your pack stayed with me?" I offered, swallowing hard as I watched him contemplate my offer.

He gazed at me with a thoughtful expression, his eyes drifting to my barely covered breasts, which were halfway covered in a towel.

I suddenly realized I was perfuming at this moment. Like a lot.

I didn't even have a chance to put on my scent-blocker lotion, and I stood embarrassed before him. I quietly hoped he wouldn't notice my smell.

But the way his nostrils flared showed that he *did* notice.

God, I smelled awful. Who wanted to smell like a bitter-smelling vegetable?

"That can work," he said finally.

We stood awkwardly for a moment as we looked at each other. Ryder's eyes darkened as he gazed at my body, and I let out a soft cough.

"Well, I better put some clothes on," I said.

"Put on your scent blocker, too," he said, and I knew my face was bright red from the warmth creeping up my cheeks. He hated my scent.

It felt like a ton of bricks crashing into my chest, and I could barely breathe from how ashamed I was.

"I know my scent is gross," I said awkwardly, staring at my bare feet. "But no need to be so rude." My eyes burned with impending tears threatening to fall. I've always been embarrassed like hell about my scent. My worst fears were coming true. Maybe it was why Jordan broke up with me.

He tilted my chin up with his finger. I wanted to be anywhere but here.

"Your scent is the complete opposite of gross," he said. "In fact, I'm holding back from completely rutting you."

What? I was so confused. My pulse was racing again now, but from arousal instead of fear.

"I smell...like ginger," I said timidly, watching as he raked my body with his gaze. My chest rose and fell rapidly as he pinned me under his gaze. His finger underneath my chin seared through my skin like a matchstick. The warmth of him near and close caused me to nearly lose it- just like in the limo.

"Then it's the best-smelling one I've ever come across," he growled, pulling his finger away from my face. "I will tell my pack of our arrangements. Put that scent blocker on immediately before you send me and the rest of the men into a rut. Before I bend you over that bed and rip that towel off. Do you understand?"

"Yes," I whispered, breathing hard.

He closed my bedroom door on his way out, and I let out another sigh. Being around him was like a storm waiting to happen. Our bodies gravitated to each other like fate, and it was something I hadn't felt with anyone before. I would have been willing if he bent me over the bed and rutted me.

The thought of it made my pussy tremble.

As I spread the scent-blocker lotion all over my body, I imagined that happening over and over again. I imagined him bending me over the bed roughly as his callused finger probed my pussy. Then, his knot stretching me to the limit. Flutters of desire roiled around my belly. God, I wanted it even though I just met him.

But he was my bodyguard.

We had to be professional- especially now that he and his pack were living with me. They were the best team they had, and I felt safe with them. The speedy response time after I called them was exactly what I needed, and I didn't want to lose them over a knot.

A knot that would feel so fucking amazing.

Ten

RYDER

I left Lacy in her room, and I was hard as a boulder as I walked down the staircase. I suddenly imagined turning around and knotting her until I could get it out of my system, but that would be reckless as hell.

"He escaped once again," said Lucas, inspecting the open window.

I was furious.

We lost the stalker again within minutes. He probably heard our armored car parking outside, even though I tried to remain discreet as possible. Listening to Lacy's scared voice over the phone put me in a state of panic and rage for the omega. Never in my heart did I feel so protective of an omega. Even though she was irresponsible and flighty, it didn't mean she deserved to be murdered in her home by a psychopath.

"He heard us coming," I muttered, staring at the shattered living room window. Lacy would have to get it repaired immediately. "Check for blood, a piece of cloth. Anything you can find."

Lucas, Adrian, and Ethan searched around the window for any evidence of him. Cooper paced the grounds with a rifle in his arms.

"What the hell does this creep want with her? Like what the

53

fuck?" said Adrian, sounding annoyed. I knew how he felt. The feeling of hopelessness and that someone had come in here just when we left her was unsettling. I rubbed my chin, leaning my elbow against the counter.

"I'm starting to think it has nothing to do with the omega disappearances," I said. "This is more on a personal level."

"I agree," said Lucas, who was inspecting the ground with a magnifying glass.

"Get that big ass thing outta here," said Adrian laughing when he saw Lucas hunched over the broken pieces of glass on his knees.

"Dude, I don't want to miss anything," said Lucas in a serious tone.

"Oh my god," Lacy gasped behind me. I turned, seeing her stare wide-eyed at her broken window. She wore cute pajamas decorated with little orange pumpkins. A pair of cotton shorts that showed off her delicious creamy thighs and her tank top revealed her tight cleavage waiting to spill. I was instantly reminded of the elusive scent she kept hidden.

The scent that called to me like no other.

My dick hardened, and I stayed behind the kitchen island so she wouldn't see the tent in my pants. She looked so innocent and frightened, walking around the devastation and staring at the shattered pieces of glass.

"You'll have to get a new window," said Ethan, turning and hugging her. My cock danced as I watched her sink into him, hugging him back. Just earlier, I had her warm body in my arms while she was naked. My breaths came out harsher, and she pulled away to look at me.

"Do you think it's a good idea for you guys to stay here?" she asked.

"Are we staying here?" asked Adrian, his eyes lighting up.

"I believe it might be the only way to ensure her safety. At least for a while," I said. "It would be mighty stupid for us to get up and leave. Unless she was coming with us."

"No, it's okay," she said. "I'll show you guys the rooms you can stay in."

"Sounds good. Let me grab Cooper here quick," I said, pulling out my phone. I called him, and he was at the house within minutes. "Anything of significance on the ground?"

"Nothing at all," said Cooper, shaking his head. His eyes were on Lacy, and I wanted to roll my eyes. My pack was getting too infatuated with her innocence and beauty. Including myself. "The stalker was careful not to leave anything behind. He's smart. For the life of me, I can't fucking figure out how he ran off so quickly."

"Not as smart as us," I said darkly. "Lacy's going to show us where we'll sleep tonight."

She was looking around at us and all the guns and weapons. If she thought this was scary, I couldn't imagine taking her to the barracks with us.

As she walked ahead of us up the stairs, I watched her little butt bouncing ahead of me. Her tiny shorts clung to her ass cheeks which made quite a sight. I looked over at Lucas and caught him staring at her ass too. Hell, my entire pack was staring. When she turned for a second, I could hear her intake of breath when she caught us all checking her out.

"Alright, so this is one of my rooms," she said, leading the way into a room covered wall-to-wall in awards.

"I want this one," said Adrian quickly, admiring the gold trophy on a dresser. "This is where it all started, right?"

"Yes," she said proudly, watching him admire her works.

"Where's my room?" I said gruffly. "We can't afford to waste time. I need my sleep so I can be up early tomorrow to investigate the cameras."

"Oh right, sorry," she said, her cheeks flushing pink. She walked us down the hallway, pointing to various rooms that were ready. Each of the men chose their room, allowing them to go ahead of me. It was the pack leader's duty to make sure his pack was taken care of. They only seemed to need a pack omega to sexually satisfy their needs and produce babies to pass on their lineage. A pack with an omega was more powerful than a pack without one.

"I'll take this one," I said, drawn to the simpleness of the room. Just a bed and a chair, which was all I needed. She bit her lip, looking around the room.

"Are you sure? I have a better one for you. You're the pack lead," she was starting to say, but I gently laid a hand on her bare upper arm. I was going to tell her not to worry, but something else took over when I touched her skin.

A rising tinge of red arose from her chest, blooming to her face at my touch. A hint of her sweet scent swirled in the air between us. Her chest rose and fell with her deep breaths as I caged her against the wall with my arms so she didn't escape.

I needed to fucking taste her. I knew she wanted it too, by how she stared up at me, fluttering her eyelashes innocently at me. The tops of her breasts were heaving up and down from her arousal. My dick responded to her scent immediately, blocking all reason.

Fuck it.

I leaned down to kiss her, wondering if she'd resist. But instead, she deepened the kiss.

Our lips met and meshed over one another. Dancing in a pattern that made my cock jump.

Her pink lips were pliant as I plundered her mouth with my tongue, tasting her. Her sweet ginger scent enveloped my very being. I felt her small hands wrap around my waist, and she pressed her body against mine. I lifted my knee, jamming it between her legs to smell her more. Her needy center, hot against my pants, made precum leak from my hardened cock. I wanted to shove my cock inside her and knot her all night until she was pregnant with my baby.

She moaned against me as I lifted my knee higher, pressing harder against her center. I craved to rip off her shorts and panties to feel her bare pussy lips rub against me. I wondered how that would feel. Her mouth tasted so good and so pliant. She tasted like mint, and I couldn't get enough.

But I had to end the kiss. She was still breathing hard and trying to rub her hot pussy against my knee.

"We're going too far, darling," I said, feeling like an ass, especially since I was the one who initiated the kiss.

She looked down ashamed, face red. "Sorry."

"Don't be sorry," I said, lowering my knee, which felt empty without her grinding on me. Cool air took its place, and I breathed in sharply to clear my mind from my racing thoughts of her. "Go to bed, Lacy. If you feel scared at all, I won't hesitate to sleep in your room tonight."

She looked like she was pondering over that. If she wanted me to sleep in her room, who knew what could happen? That type of temptation was too much, and I wouldn't be able to resist shacking up in her bed with my knot hard and fast inside her.

"I..." she started to say. "I think I'm okay. As long as you guys are here, I feel a lot safer. I don't want things to go too far either."

"Good," I said, and she looked disappointed as she bit her lower lip. "After tonight, no distractions, okay?"

It was much harder said than done. To put an alpha and omega alone in a room together was a recipe for disaster.

"Yes, we'll be professional," she said, and I gave her a peck on the cheek.

"Perfect," I said. "Be a good girl now and go to bed."

Her face reddened even more at my praise of her, and I knew she secretly liked it by the trail of her scent as she left the room. She hadn't even left the room before I started unbuckling my belt and letting my pants drop. She jumped and turned- her eyes widening at my hard cock standing at attention.

She opened her mouth and closed it again, staring at my member. The only thing her mouth should be doing was sucking me off, I thought dryly. I smiled when she turned and hurried to her room after filling up my room with her scent of arousal.

Stripping off all my clothes, I lay on the bed with a groan. At forty, my body was already aching in places that shouldn't. The only place that should ache was my cock. I gripped my cock and closed my eyes, imagining the omega giving me a massage ending with my cock in her mouth.

But just as I thought that I felt something wet clamp onto my cock. Opening my eyes, I saw Lacy sitting in my bed with her lips around my dick. *Oh fuck.* My ball sack tightened as I watched her eyes turn dreamy as she pulled my cock into her mouth even deeper.

Her tongue swirled around the tip of my cock covered in precum.

"Lacy, this isn't a good idea," I groaned, trying not to explode in her mouth. She grasped my thighs, her nails digging into my skin. It was her way of telling me to shut up, and I wasn't going to argue.

I leaned on my elbows, watching her suck me off. Her innocent eyes were wide when my cock grew another two inches in her mouth. Her wet lips tightened around me, and her mouth suctioned me down her throat while her tongue swirled around my tip.

"Fuck," I growled, watching the open door. Anyone could come in and see her sucking off my cock. But there was no way in hell I was stopping her now. I gripped her hair and gyrated my hips against her mouth. "You're a dirty little omega, aren't you? Did you secretly want my knot deep inside your hot little cunt?"

She moaned greedily around my cock, as I gripped her hair even tighter. I bucked, orgasming into her mouth. She swallowed quickly, not letting a drop hit the bed. She licked me from my shaft to the tip of my cock as I tried to catch my breath. All the tension seemed to release from my shoulders after her attentive care. She released my cock from her mouth and looked at me with uncertainty.

Then she gave me a naughty smile.

"Sleep tight, pack leader," she said to me, her breath catching when I grasped her breast in my hand.

"I sure will, but we can't do this again, Lacy," I said. "Unless you want my knot inside you? And you'll be round with my baby."

"Maybe that's what I want," she breathed, and I squeezed her breast until she yelped.

"Let's catch your stalker first, and then I can think about that," I said.

"Then you better do it fast," she said, making my balls tighten again at the thought of claiming her as my omega.

Eleven

LACY

The next morning, I was sitting cross-legged on my bed in shock at what happened last night.

Did I seriously just give the head of my security a fucking blowjob?!

I didn't have anything to drink last night, but somehow, everything felt like a dream - like I was drugged. Did an alpha's scent have that kind of effect on omegas? But I never felt that with my ex-boyfriend, so maybe not.

But it could be a possibility.

Today was going to be a late start to work. I had a singing gig with my band at a wedding at five today. The couple paid us a big chunk of money to play at their wedding, and I was excited. And the bodyguards would have to accompany me. I almost groaned with embarrassment at the thought. I never thought I'd be prancing around with personal bodyguards and being one of *those* celebrities.

Shit, I needed to make breakfast for everyone.

I rubbed my eyes and walked into the bathroom connected to my room. I washed my face, brushed, and tied my hair up in a messy bun until I could shower after breakfast and prepare for the wedding.

I still wore my pajamas from last night as I walked down the stairs. I wasn't prepared to see a bunch of guns lying on the couches while Lucas cleaned them. He looked up at me with a smile that barely reached his eyes. I briefly wondered who hurt him in his past. He was just so serious *all* the freaking time.

"Morning, Lucas," I said, sitting on the armchair beside him. His attention was diverted back to the gun as he wiped it down with a rag. "Did you sleep good?"

"I did, thank you," he said, not looking at me. His one silver earring that dangled from his ear caught the sunlight, and I studied the weathered lines on his face.

"That's good," I said, not knowing what else to say to him. He wasn't one for conversation. "Would you like breakfast?"

"Sure."

"What would you like to eat?"

"Anything you have. I'm not very picky," he said gruffly, rubbing a hand over his buzz cut. His tattoos looked fierce all over his arms. He wore a simple white tank top and sweatpants. I guess the guards had an off time and didn't always wear suits.

Then I remembered Ryder in bed last night, and my face turned hot. He most definitely wasn't wearing a suit.

"Okay, I'll make scrambled eggs then," I said, getting up and walking to the kitchen. Grabbing the egg carton from the fridge, I cracked as many eggs as I had left into the mixing bowl. I didn't go shopping much for myself, just the bare minimum since I lived alone.

But now I had no idea how long these men would be staying at my house.

"Let me help you, dear," said Ethan, appearing beside me and gently tugging the whisk from my hand. He was wearing his suit already, and I wondered if he slept in it. His short beard looked rugged from sleep, but he looked content.

"Thank you," I said, handing him the bowl as he whisked it furiously. "You look like an alpha who knows his way around the kitchen."

"I don't know much about cooking, to be honest," he chuckled. "How did you sleep, Miss Lacy?"

"Much better now that you're all here," I said, looking for a large pan. "It would be impossible for anyone to get to me. Or for anyone to break into my house."

"That's very true," he said, salting the eggs in the bowl. I put the pan on the stove and watched him pour the mixture in. "But you still need to be careful."

"You don't have to help with breakfast," I said.

"This is no trouble at all. We're the ones inconveniencing you, my dear," he said. My stomach flipped every time he called me that. He had an older gentleman-like demeanor, and somehow, I trusted him instinctively.

The gentle quiet of our cooking was interrupted when Adrian came down the stairs yawning loudly and only wearing a pair of black briefs. His tanned chest had impeccable definition from his muscles.

"Hey, Lacy," said Adrian, leaning against the fridge. I tried not to stare because whenever we looked at each other, my heart would beat out of control. His wild abandon made me want to drop everything and run off into the sunset with him. He was the fun one, and I knew hanging out with him would be trouble.

"Where's your clothes?" I said briskly, grabbing the bacon slices from the freezer. "Did you lose it on your way here?"

"I did," said Adrian, grabbing a jug of milk from the refrigerator like it was his house. My eyes widened when I watched him chug down a whole glass in front of me. "Yes, I'm an alpha with a big appetite."

"I can see that," I said, watching as he washed the glass in the sink, his elbow brushing mine. The contact sent flurries of desire to flow through me. For an omega, it was natural for me to gravitate to more than one alpha until the pack marked me as theirs with their bites.

The men were all sitting around the table, myself included, with scrambled eggs and bacon.

"Sorry, the meal isn't fancier," I said. "This is all I had today."

"This is perfect," said Lucas, his mouth full as he dug into his plate with gusto. I was sitting between him and Cooper. Ryder was sitting across from me, oddly silent as he ate each bite as if pondering over something in his mind.

Nervousness and apprehension settled within me as I ate. I started to wonder if last night was a figment of my imagination. He wasn't looking at me in the eyes, and all he wanted to talk about was business.

The nervousness in me was slowly forming into hurt. I never thought he'd be like other alphas, stringing me along with my emotions only to break my heart afterward.

"Did you check the cameras, Ryder?" asked Adrian.

"Fuck," said Ryder, dropping his fork onto place with a clatter. He slapped his forehead and shook his head. "I was completely distracted."

"We think we know why," said Adrian, chuckling as he ate. My face burned as Adrian looked between Ryder and me.

"Shut your mouth," barked Ryder, and I jumped.

For some reason, I sat there hurt. *Was it really that bad that I had given him probably the best blowjob of his life? Or maybe it was terrible.*

The men didn't say a word as they watched Ryder get up from the table to check out his laptop on the coffee table. We could all tell he was grumpy this morning.

I watched, too, wondering if he could give us a definite description of my stalker. But as I watched, I felt like a prostitute or some cheap omega. Him not looking me in the eyes or acknowledging me this morning was embarrassing.

I followed the pack to the living room to see what Ryder pulled up on the laptop. I didn't want to, but I had to show that he didn't affect me. He growled in frustration as he watched plain static on the screen.

"The fucker disconnected the camera somehow," said Ethan,

inspecting the wires and high up on the ladder to check the camera. "Yeah, he disconnected a wire."

"Replace the wire, and we'll install more cameras around the house," said Ryder. Then he turned to me. "What time are we leaving for the studio?"

"We're not going to the studio. Later at five, I have to perform at a wedding," I said stonily, not looking at him. He didn't get the right to talk to me whenever he wanted to. I could feel his gaze on my face as I spoke. "Everyone is free to do whatever until then."

"Cool," said Ryder, his gaze returning to the laptop.

"I'll buy groceries for us," said Cooper amidst the awkwardness.

His pack leader clearly couldn't stand my presence after last night. Maybe he couldn't stand my scent. After a while my scent could get sickening, I thought, with my stomach dropping at the thought.

I walked to the table and started to clear it up with Adrian's help. Adrian seemed to notice the tension between Ryder and I since he was trying to crack light jokes. I just wasn't in the mood.

"Thanks, Adrian, I got the dishes now. I prefer to wash it alone," I said.

"Got ya," he said. "I guess I should shower and put some clothes on."

"Okay," I said, unable to crack a smile. He lingered in the kitchen after my short response, and then he finally left me alone, bounding up the stairs to get ready. As I washed the dishes, lost in my thoughts, I saw someone standing next to me drying off the dishes for me. I looked to my right to see Ryder calmly wiping a plate with a dry rag.

I never asked for his help.

I would rather much prefer being in the kitchen alone. Tense silence reigned between us. His body near mine sent signals to my omega wolf that the pack leader was nearby. My breathing came out harsher and faster as I washed the dishes, willing him to go away in my mind.

"It's okay, I got this," I said tersely, gritting my teeth.

"Is there something wrong?" he asked. The nerve of him. *Why was he acting like he wasn't the one with the attitude this morning? What the hell was wrong with this alpha?*

But as I washed another glass- I dropped it, and it shattered in the sink with a small crash.

Shit.

I dipped my hand into the sink to pick up the large piece.

"Don't!" said Ryder.

But it was too late, and the palm of my hand was bleeding everywhere. The impending sharp pain hit me two seconds later, and I howled in agony, washing my hand under the running water and gripping my injured hand with my other one.

"Ahh," I said as Ryder grabbed my wrist and pulled it away from the water.

"It'll just keep bleeding," he said. "Lucas, see if there's anything in our van, please."

"On it," he said gruffly, slamming the front door open as he ran out.

The pain was sharp as a knife across the long cut on my skin as Ryder pressed a paper towel onto my wound. We stood there like that, gaze on my hand -refusing to look at him. His large, callused hand wrapped around my wrist seemed to relieve some of the pain.

Or maybe it was my brain playing tricks on me.

Twelve

RYDER

I tried to remain cordial and professional with Lacy this morning.

We were getting into dangerous territory, especially after last night. But now, with her hand in mine and her beautiful scent overwhelming me- I obviously did a lousy job since she was here now, standing before me, angry and in pain.

"I can handle it," she gritted out.

She winced as I pulled the paper towel off.

"I'm going to cool your wound with my tongue," I assured her, pressing my tongue against the palm of her hand. I watched her wince in pain again as I licked the angry scar on her palm. Her scent made my soul come alive. Her very essence intoxicated me, and the intimate act caused all the blood flow to go down to my groin.

I gazed at her, studying her flushed face. She looked unsure, but the smell between her legs signaled to me that she was aroused. Her ever-sweet ginger scent that she was afraid of. It was the cutest thing.

"I only found bandages," said Lucas, rushing back into the kitchen with the box in his hands.

"The worst of it is over," I said, peeling a bandage and gently pressing it onto her palm. "How do you feel, Lacy?"

"It's okay," she said, her eyes on the shattered glass in the sink.

"I'll take care of the rest of it," I assured her, and she nodded, hesitantly pulling her soft hand from mine.

"Thank you," she said, still not looking at me in the eyes. She was still angry at me, but it was for the best. We couldn't get entangled like this for her safety. When she walked away, I watched her cute bottom swinging in front of me as she walked seductively upstairs.

"You need to be more patient with her," commented Lucas, looking at me sideways. He had seen me checking her out. Besides Ethan, I had known Lucas the longest. He was quiet, but he was observant and kept to himself. Loyal to the pack and never spilled any secrets.

"You're right, Lucas," I said. "It's becoming tougher to control myself being around her."

"I can barely talk around her," said Lucas. "All I think about is knotting the fuck out of her."

"You never talk, Lucas," joked Ethan, strolling into the kitchen and combing his beard with his fingers. I cleaned up the rest of the glass and rinsed off the sink for Lacy. I didn't want her hurting herself again.

"The outdoor wedding sounds like it'll be fun," said Adrian, also joining us.

"Did you say outdoors?" I asked as I dried my hands with a towel. This wasn't good. An outdoor event was not safe at all. I imagined her on stage...if someone shot her, I would never forgive myself. The stark image of blood blossoming over her white blazer struck fear in my heart for her.

We still hadn't caught the jackass following her around yet. It wasn't safe.

"Yes, I looked into the event," said Adrian. "Do you think she'll let us dance with her? I want to hold her in my arms so fucking bad."

"No, that can't happen," I said. My chest pumped furiously as I paced the kitchen. Memories of the last omega I've ever had to guard years ago flashed through me, making me sick.

"Dude, she's going to hate you so bad," said Adrian.

"Don't do it, Ryder," said Ethan. "She'll fucking fire us."

"No. The contract states that if we deem her safety is at risk, then we have the right to hold her back from events like this," I explained. "If she doesn't comply, she'll be barred from hiring anyone from our company."

"Shit, she's gonna be pissed," said Adrian, shaking his head. "Good luck."

"Thanks, I could use it," I said, listening to her singing loudly in the shower. We all quieted down to listen to her beautiful, melodic voice that put us all in a trance. If an omega's scent captivated me, her voice pulled me even more.

I had no idea how she would take the news.

I hoped she wouldn't fire us and risk her life in the process. And she was a fiery, strong-headed omega on top of that, so I had no idea what to expect.

Thirteen

LACY

I was giddy with excitement as I got ready for the wedding.
Deep down, I was excited for my bodyguards to listen to me singing and share in my personal life. I felt something towards them- Ryder especially. The memory of him licking my hand caused me to tremble in the shower and use my handy vibrator. Being around a hulking alpha like him caused my lady parts to go haywire.

I slathered on the scent blocker lotion all over my body. I had to make sure I was covered. Every inch of me. I didn't want to take any chances tonight with the bodyguards. At any moment, I was scared I would give in and beg for a knot, but I couldn't. Taking a heat suppressant pill every morning as soon as I woke up ensured I wouldn't go into heat. A baby would derail my career and end all chances of success after all my hard work. I pulled on white underwear and a bra to wear with the dress I picked out for tonight.

It was a beautiful dress, and my heart fluttered as I picked it up. When I put it on, I turned to the mirror as I tied the sash into a ribbon in the back. It was a purple dress studded with gems across the cleavage portion. The material flowed down to my ankles and swirled around my gold strappy heels. After doing my makeup and hair, I spritzed some perfume to cover up any gingery scent that could emit from me.

I loved my look today and couldn't wait to meet the guys downstairs so we could go. I carefully stepped down the wooden stairs to avoid slipping with my heels on. I was mildly disappointed when I didn't see all the guys right away.

It was just Ryder standing at my front door.

He looked nervous as he gazed at me, his hands clasped behind him. His shirt bulged with his muscular frame underneath, sending a flurry of desire through me.

"Ryder?" I said, stepping down the last step. I tried not to trip on my feet as I walked towards him. His gaze made me feel naked and exposed as he looked at me. But I could feel his nervous energy, and I wanted to know what happened. *Had the stalker come back for me?*

"Lacy," he said. "I have to tell you something."

"What is it?" I asked. "Did he come back? The stalker, I mean."

"No, nothing like that," he replied, and my breathing eased a little at that. "You can't go today to your wedding event."

I took a deep breath. I was unsure of what the hell he was trying to say.

"Excuse me?"

"It's an outdoor event, and you must remain low-key as much as possible," he explained. My heart was rapidly beating in a panic. "At least for a few days. The stalker is still actively trying to come after you. He's desperate, and this event would be the perfect opportunity for him to do something particularly nasty."

"But that's what I have *you* for, right?" I said, trying to keep calm. There was no way in hell he had the power to make me stay home today. I was all dressed and excited to go. Anger bubbled in my chest, threatening to spill over in one big fighting match.

"That's right, but we can't control many factors if this is

outdoors," he said prepared. As if he knew I was going to challenge him.

"Well, I'm not staying home today if that's what you're thinking," I said. "Can you move, please? I need to get to the limo."

"I'm sorry," he said, not moving an inch.

My heart started to race.

"Oh really? Do you want to be fired?" I challenged. I couldn't believe the nerve of him. It was killing me every second I was forced to stay here.

I needed to do my job.

"If you fire me, you won't be able to hire any bodyguards," he stated.

"That's fine. I don't need you guys," I huffed adamantly. "Move. Now."

"The stalker was in your house last night," he reminded me. "What if we hadn't come and scared him off?"

Fuck. I forgot about that already. Without them, I would've been toast. But I wasn't going down without a fight. I started running towards the back door and around the kitchen. Ethan was standing at that door with a grim look.

"No!" I screamed, trying to push him aside so I could leave.

"I apologize, my dear," he said as I pushed and shoved at his hard chest. His body felt like fucking granite, and I was starting to get tired.

"Please, this is important to me," I begged. "I can't call them and cancel. I can't do this."

"You can," said Ethan.

I wanted to scream, cry, or break something. Panic and anger ballooned inside me, ready to explode. I ran around every entrance, and there was a guard in front of each one. Even Adrian was blocking the exit that led to my swimming pool.

"I'm sorry, Lacy," he said, grabbing my arms when I tried to swing at him. His strong arms encircled me, and my eyes burned with tears.

"Adrian, please let me out."

"Pack leader's orders," he said softly, purring into my neck. I pulled away, not wanting to be comforted.

"Fuck you all," I shouted as I ran up the stairs. With tears blurring my vision, I ran down the hallway and burst into my nesting room. I slammed the door behind me, ripped off my heels, and threw them against the wall. My hands shook as I dropped my purse onto the central nest in the middle of the room. It was one giant pink cushion surrounded by little pink pillows.

I usually came in here when I wasn't feeling good or depressed.

Breathing hard, I paced around the room, clutching my phone. I didn't have a choice but to cancel. I had to call Ben or Ty. This was all too much for me to handle right now.

I let out a frustrated yell, throwing a pillow against the wall.

I dropped my phone and gripped another pillow, tearing the cloth apart. I was on a complete rampage as I ripped apart the pillows, feathers flying everywhere as they lay scattered. I yelled again as I ripped into the floor cushions next. All I saw was red. I didn't care about anything.

The stalker ruined my life.

All the freedom I worked hard for- he ruined. I wanted to rip his head off his body. I wanted to go outside and confront this jerk. I pulled the window open and looked out. It was a long way down to the ground. I would die if I tried jumping out. The cool air hit my face as I stood at the window, gripping the frame of it with my bloodied hands. The bandage had come off, and blood was all over. I didn't give a fuck anymore.

I was all perfect and ready to sing until they stopped me. And firing my bodyguards would make sure the stalker won.

"Fuck you," I said out loud, gazing at the fountain in my backyard. Taking deep breaths, my anger dissipated, now replaced with sadness. It would be foolish not to listen to the bodyguards after their many years of experience.

I usually didn't give a fuck about my own safety. But I had to now. While standing at the window, the cool air on my hot face gave me some clarity. My breaths started to slow as I calmed down.

I had to think rationally. I couldn't be impulsive anymore.

Removing myself from the window, I walked back to my phone on the ground, which was lost amongst a bunch of pink pillows and feathers. I didn't even want to look back at the disaster I created.

I dialed Ben's number. He would be easier to talk to at a time like this.

"Lacy, what's going on?" he asked. "You're late as fuck."

"I know, I can't come," I said. My hand trembled in pain, and I knew my phone was covered in blood now.

"Are you joking or serious? What are you talking about?"

"The stalker broke into my house, and the bodyguards think I should sit this one out," I explained. I just wanted to get this over with quickly. This conversation was way too painful for me. More painful than the cut on my hand.

"What's going on?" I heard Ty ask in the background and Ben muttering the news to him. "Lacy, just fire them. You're the star of the show."

"Just do it without me," I said. "Ty, you can sing solo."

"The guests will be so fucking upset you're not here," said Ty. "But fine. Next week, we want to see you at work. Your bodyguards better do their damn jobs and catch the asshole ruining our lives."

"I know," I sighed. "I'm so sorry, guys."

"It's okay, Lacy," said Ben. "I know you don't like this. We know how dedicated you are to the team. Don't sweat it, okay?"

"Okay," I said, my voice trembling as I hung up. I threw the phone down as I collapsed onto the giant cushion, crying. Tears flowed down my face, drenching the pillow tucked underneath my chin.

I hated disappointing my fans. I didn't want to cancel, but I had to.

My body was weak and worn out now after my tirade. I tried fighting each bodyguard and got nowhere. I tried everything I could to leave and sing at the wedding. The door slowly opened, and I recognized Ryder's black socks lined in red as he stood before me.

Fourteen

LACY

Ryder's large frame rested next to mine as he sat next to me on the round, fluffy cushion. I could see the gold watch on his hand flashing as he tapped his knee, watching me silently. We sat for a few minutes in silence until he cleared his throat.

I sniffled, and he handed me a napkin. I grabbed it roughly and blew my nose.

"I'm sorry, Lacy," he said simply. "You've destroyed your nest honey. Why did you do that?"

"Singing is my dream," I said. "You have no idea what you did to me."

"Your hand," he said, grabbing my hand, and we both stared at the line of blood leaking. He licked my palm, and I gasped at the roughness of his tongue. The feeling sent desire flowing through me immediately at the impact. He grabbed another bandage from his pocket and quickly taped me up again.

"Why do you even care?"

"I would rather you stay alive than end up..."

"End up dead? I'm paying you money anyway," I said, gripping the tissue in my hand as I stared at the pattern of the cushions.

"I'm not doing this for the money," he said slowly.

I looked up and saw that he was lost in his thoughts as he played with a piece of feather on the ground.

"Then what is it? Why do you care?"

"Because I care about you," he said. "And it's for my sanity."

"What do you mean?" I sighed.

"Years ago," he started. "I was supposed to guard an omega from her family. She wouldn't tell me why."

I couldn't imagine why an omega would want to be protected from her own family. I was lucky my family would literally die for me if anything happened.

"What happened?" I asked, my curiosity piqued.

"I walked her to her college, but when I came back to pick her up," he said. "Reyna was gone. I found out her parents had auctioned her off. I don't know what became of her. I wasn't strict enough on her."

"Oh," I said as chills went through me. This was when Omega Auctions were legal, which had now been outlawed. "I...that's horrible. Did you have...feelings for Reyna?"

"I did not. And I don't want anything bad to happen to you," he said, gazing at me with a dark expression. "If anything happened to you, I would go mad. I never felt more inadequate after that day and tried to leave my job. But my boss wouldn't hear of it. Imagine someone trusting you with their life, and then you disappoint them. I have no idea what became of her."

I bit my lip.

"I'll try my best, Ryder," I said finally. "I'll try to cooperate, but I can't keep doing this and disappoint my fans."

"I understand," he said. "It's not something that will happen a lot, I promise. We just need to be cautious."

"How about tomorrow then?" I asked. "There's a baby shower I have to go to. I already bought presents, and my cousin is coming over tomorrow to go with me."

"That's fine," he said. "I don't have a problem with that, and it's indoors."

"Well, thank god," I said, and he wiped a tear from my cheek with his thumb.

"I don't like seeing you cry," he said. "You should feel happy, protected, and safe with me."

"I feel safe but definitely not happy."

"Don't be a brat, Lacy."

"I'm not," I pouted, throwing a pillow at him with all my force. Some of the feathers stuck in his hair, and I tried to keep a straight face. He sat there looking momentarily shocked, unable to believe that I dared throw a pillow at the pack leader.

But he wasn't *my* leader.

"Why did you throw that at me?" he said simply, unmoving as he watched me calmly. But I could see the brewing storm behind his eyes.

"This morning, you pretended I didn't exist. What the hell was that about?"

"I didn't want to confuse you," he said.

"You're not making any sense."

"I want to keep things professional because you would never want to be with a bodyguard like myself," he said. "We don't belong together. You're a celebrity, and what am I?"

Butterflies swirled in my belly at his statement. He was fighting his feelings.

But he had *feelings*.

"You're right," I said in a low voice, not wanting to make things awkward. I didn't want babies or anything like that, so I needed to keep things professional, too. But at the same time, I saw nothing wrong with us wanting to be together if we wanted to. Sure, it'd create a splash on the news, but I didn't care.

He touched the small of my back and hugged me from the side. I leaned into him, feeling his warmth on my body and wishing he didn't make so much sense all the time. He wasn't a bad alpha. He was trying to protect me. To protect my feelings and my physical well-being.

And I respected him for it.

"It's for the best little omega," he whispered.

～

THE NEXT DAY, I was sitting quietly as everyone chattered away at the baby shower. I was still bummed about missing out on my singing gig. And when Ben told me about getting booed on stage, it upset me.

"Lacy, why don't you take part in the challenges?" asked Alana gently as she sat next to me. Her belly was round with her third child, and her eyes glittered with excitement as she watched the crowded room. She looked beautiful in her flowing emerald dress with the braided shoulder straps, complimenting her golden skin. "Is something the matter?"

"No," I said, forcing a smile on my face.

"Do you want your bodyguards to leave my house? I can kick them out for you, don't worry. I can see you looking at them, annoyed and all."

"No, it's okay. I'm just a little hungry, that's all," I said.

Alana and I reconnected after her wedding. For years after high school, Alana didn't speak to anyone and even avoided me. I attributed it to life getting in the way and everyone going down different paths in life. But I did wonder what happened to her, and she finally told me after her honeymoon. I felt sad for her when she told me about her attack, but I was glad she had found her men who'd do anything to protect her.

"Oh, okay! Have some snacks then," she said, patting my arm. "There's a table full of them."

"Sounds good," I said, getting up. But as I stood up, her two-year-old son Jay barreled towards me and wrapped his little arms around my knees. His round, amber-glowing eyes and dark hair were a stark contrast against the paleness of his skin since his father was a vampire. "Jay! I missed you."

He laughed with delight when I picked up him and walked to the snack table with him. He pointed to the green jello in a cup, and I grabbed it for him in a heartbeat. Whatever he wanted, I gave him. I considered myself an auntie to him and his twin sister, June, who was napping.

"Yummy," he said when he clumsily stabbed the jello with the plastic spoon. I craved to have a baby of my own one day, especially when I spent time with him. He brought out the baby fever in me even though he was a handful.

While he was on my shoulder, I made my own plate, trying not to bump into people. I just threw a few cookies on there to look like I was doing something. I felt off today and didn't feel like celebrating anything. But it was Alana's special day, and I needed to get it together.

I released Jay, and he ran toward his mother with the jello cup in his hands, and I smiled. Maybe that was what I needed to feel better about yesterday.

"Game time!" shouted Olivia. She had helped Alana a lot with arranging the baby shower.

There weren't any males in the room except for my bodyguards. There was a row of chairs and a table in front of it with baby dolls. Diapers were sitting next to them. "The first one to successfully put a diaper on a doll wins the game! Who wants to come up?"

I looked at my bodyguards and saw Ethan whispering to Ryder with a smirk on his face.

"They can do it," I said, pointing a finger at them.

Ryder's eyebrows went up as he rubbed his head nervously. Ethan shook his head.

"Nope," said Ethan. "We're only here to guard ya."

"I think that's a fantastic idea," said Olivia, winking at me. She knew how annoyed I was last night, and this was the perfect revenge. Ryder seemed to notice this when he gave me a dark look as he sat on his chair. Ethan shuffled his feet, but he reluctantly took a seat next to Ryder. "Here are your blindfolds."

I watched, giggling as they were blindfolded by the vicious Olivia. Three more contestants sat at the table to join.

"Is it time?" asked Ethan, reaching for the diaper.

"Not yet," Olivia snapped at him, and my smile grew wider. The way they were all smug guarding the doors of my home to block *me* from leaving wasn't something I could get over easily.

Surprisingly, Ryder was deft with his hands and quick when he quickly put the diaper on the doll. Ethan fumbled and managed to wrap it around the doll's head, to everyone's amusement. The timer dinged, and they all took off their blindfolds. Ryder smiled triumphantly at me, holding the doll up like a trophy. I rolled my eyes.

"Looks like I won. What's the prize?" asked Ryder cockily.

"You'll be the first to choose the flavor you'd like to try for the baby foods. It's guess-the-flavor game next," said Olivia.

"Hmm, I'll pass on that one," said Ryder, trying to be polite. "Listen, we need to take a walk around the premises. It was nice meeting you all."

"It was nice meeting you, too," said Olivia, smiling widely.

"We'll be outside waiting for you, Lacy," said Ethan, hastily getting up as well. At that, they both flew out the door.

I laughed, taking a bite out of the giant cookie.

"Well, that got rid of them," said Alana.

"You're a genius, Olivia," I said.

I walked into the kitchen to throw away my plate and saw Olivia's mother, Jade, and Alana's mother, Tiana, speaking in hushed voices in there. Their whispers were hushed and urgent. I tried not to be obvious as I eavesdropped. I was always the nosy one among the kids when we were young.

Oh, they were talking about another omega gone missing...

Damn. Things were really serious.

"Hello, Lacy," said my aunt Jade. "Long time no see."

"Hey, Auntie," I said. I had known them since I was little, and they were like second mothers to me, so I was comfortable talking to them. "I couldn't help but overhear you talking."

"Yes, it's so sad," said Tiana, shaking her head. "There's someone or something out there targeting omegas."

"I mean, it isn't new," said Jade. "Over the dawn of time, we were targets of alphas and every creature alive."

"Be careful out there, Lacy," said Tiana, earnestly grabbing my hand. "The world is not as rosy and pretty as you think it might be."

Fifteen

RYDER

After getting back from the dreadful baby shower, I watched Lacy from the staircase as she lay on Adrian's lap, sleeping soundly while a movie played in the living room. Cooper, Ethan, and Adrian were all knocked out after the festivities. I wanted to investigate but couldn't tear my eyes away from Lacy's sleeping form. She wore another cute pair of pajamas that flattered her curvy ass and hips.

Fuck, I wanted to scoop her up in my arms and drop her on the bed. I wanted to see her cheeks flush as I knotted her over and over again. My dick started coming to life, begging to sink into her soft pliant pussy.

No, I couldn't do that to her.

Ripping my gaze away from her sleeping form, I focused instead on the task at hand. I walked down the hall and stopped at her room. I knelt in front of the door, looking for any clue or traces that Lacy's stalker must have left behind when he broke in. I inspected every piece of dirt I could find. Snapping on gloves, I placed any viable evidence into a small plastic bag. Before turning to leave, something caught my eye.

Lacy's pink panties were hanging off the side of the laundry basket. I knew what they were judging from the lace at the edges. My heart pounded faster in my chest as I stared at it. This was her private room. I shouldn't be in here. But I slowly pulled my gloves off and stuffed it in my pocket.

Just a peek.

I walked into her room, and with my back facing the door, I carefully picked up her lace pink panties between my fingers. I felt like the biggest creep in the world right now. But fuck it, I couldn't stay away from her scent. A whiff of her pussy wafted, and my heart beat faster. All the blood rushed down to my cock. I opened the panties up, looking at the seat of it. There was a dark stain, and it was still wet between my bare fingers.

Fuck yes.

I lifted the seat of her panties to my nose and inhaled deeply. Fuck. She smelled so fucking good. A stronger scent of ginger but muted with her strong pussy smell. Inhaling again, I jammed my hand down my sweatpants, gripping my cock.

∾

WHEN I WOKE UP, I felt something pressing against my mouth.

Opening my eyes, confused- I saw that Adrian's hard cock was in my mouth as he snored above me. Thankfully, he was wearing pants. I didn't realize that I had fallen asleep on him. *Oh my god*, I gently moved the tip of his dick out of my mouth, and he didn't stir. Looking around, I saw that the rest of the pack was knocked out and couldn't stay awake to watch the movie.

I grabbed the remote and switched the television off.

Hearing something, I slowly walked up the stairs. It sounded like someone was grunting. The sound of the grunts grew louder the nearer I went to my room. When I peeked my head around the door, I held a hand to my mouth in shock.

I couldn't believe what I was seeing.

Ryder's back was facing me, but I could see the pink panties that I ripped off earlier today stuffed into his mouth. He was grunting heavily as he gripped his penis beneath his pants. I could see the movement of his hand underneath his pants. Shock flowed through me, and I didn't know how to feel about it. My body naturally responded to the sight, slick instantly drenching between my thighs. My breathing quickened, and my brain screamed at me to leave.

Ryder's hand instantly stopped, and he turned, seeing me at the door.

My face heated as I stood there. I wanted to leave, but I didn't want to at the same time.

"Wha...what are you doing?" I whispered.

He stood there breathing hard, his eyes darkening with lust as he gazed at me.

He dropped the panties back into the laundry basket and stalked toward me as I stood there wide-eyed. He leaned his face down to my neck and brought his mouth to my ear, nibbling on my earlobe.

"What if I could taste the real thing? Just one lick."

Oh god.

My brain screamed at me to run, but my trembling pussy made the decision for me.

"Yes," I said, my voice barely above a whisper. I gasped when he silently lifted me off the floor and deposited me onto the bed. My thighs were trembling as he separated them. I was still wearing my shorts, but he didn't care as he pressed his nose between my legs. My heart pounded faster and faster as I felt his nose rubbing against my pussy. I was worried about how I'd smell after taking a nap.

"Fuck, I want to knot you so bad," he said.

"I want it, Ryder," I said, my voice a sob as my pussy clenched. I wanted him deep inside me. To knot me and sate me until I was fucking satisfied for once. I was done being a virgin today.

"Tell me how much you want it, baby," he said, rubbing his nose harder and faster against my pussy.

"I want you deep inside me. I want to be stretched like never before," I said. "I want you to be my first."

A look of pure primal energy came over him.

"I will be your first," he said, lifting himself over me. "And your last."

I bit my lip shyly as he peeled off my shorts and underwear. My breaths came out in short gasps when I was exposed to him. Nervousness set in, and all my bravery shot out the window when he carefully separated my thighs while I was naked. Only my breasts were covered now from my tank top. He kissed my knees and my thighs. I shivered underneath him in anticipation. His kisses trailed upward to my pussy as he kissed my pussy lips, traveling and exploring with his mouth.

I never thought such a delight existed.

But when his tongue shot out to lick my clitoris, my belly clenched. My pussy released more slick, and I was embarrassed at the strong smell.

"I'm sorry about the smell," I whispered.

His thick tongue lapped up my pussy, flicking my clit with the tip of his tongue. The flicks of his tongue against my enlarged clit sent vibrational waves through my body. My stomach clenched in desire when he did it over and over.

"Never apologize. You taste like ginger candy," he said, flicking my clit again and I moaned. All thoughts of the other men hearing us went out the door. All I wanted was release. He flicked his tongue harder against my clit, and then he sucked on me so hard until I shook and shuddered. "Taste yourself. See how good you fucking taste omega."

Then he leaned over me and pressed his lips to mine. I was curious about what he meant by ginger candy.

I tasted myself on his lips as we kissed. He was right about my taste. It wasn't as bitter and gross as I imagined. A strong undertone of sweetness hit my tongue when he pressed his lips to mine. His strong alpha pheromones sent my brain into a whirl. His unrelenting cock had come out of his pants, pressing against the entrance of my pussy.

He broke the kiss and gazed at me with hesitation.

"I want this," I said.

"I don't want you to feel pressured for your first time," he said.

"Trust me, I don't," I said earnestly, widening my legs under him. I wanted to know how it felt to have a cock deep inside me. "I've been a virgin long enough. I need someone to break it. If not you, then Adrian."

He growled.

"*I* will take your virginity and knot you until you can no longer handle it," he grunted, pressing his dick against the entrance of my pussy. Every inch of him stretched me as he slowly pushed inside me.

All of a sudden, a sharp pain pressed between my legs, and I yelped as I felt his thick cock break my hymen in one go.

"Oh, Ryder," I gasped. He stopped instantly, studying my face with strained breaths.

"Are you okay, Lacy?" he asked with concern. The stress of holding back was evident on his face.

"I'm okay," I said, taking deep breaths. The pain was slowly dwindling away even though it was still there. I didn't want his pulsing cock to stop.

He stretched me wider as he pushed deeper inside me, slowly thrusting in and out. The dark room was silent except for our harsh breathing colliding. The bed squeaked with every powerful thrust into my pussy. I moaned as he pressed his lips to mine, and he jammed his tongue into my mouth as he fucked me on my pink bed.

"I'm going to knot your little pussy soon," he growled against my mouth.

"Okay," I whimpered, closing my eyes as he thrust over and

over into me. Pounding into my pussy. My pussy clenched and released slick, easing the movement of his cock inside of me. The tension in my belly rose from arousal when that happened. I started to feel more pleasure, enjoying his cock inside me more.

Just the way I imagined it to happen.

His tongue in my mouth grew more urgent, mimicking the movements of his cock inside me.

"You're so fucking tight, I love taking your virginity," he said. Then he growled against my collarbone as he released copious amounts of semen inside me. I wasn't worried about getting pregnant because of my heat suppressants.

My heart pounded hard, nervous about my first knot.

We locked eyes as his dick swelled to an impossible proportion inside my pussy. His cock kept getting bigger within me when I thought it would stop.

"Oh no," I said. "It's not stopping. You're still swelling!"

"That's supposed to happen, baby," he said, bringing his face down to purr into my neck. "It's very normal. Your body was made for me. You can handle the knot. Relax your mind and body."

My pussy was being stretched as I lay underneath him, trying to take him all in. His penis swelled even more until I cried out. And at that point, it mercifully stopped. All I felt now was a giant hot dog-shaped balloon stuffed into my pussy, locking me to this huge alpha bodyguard with intense green eyes and a scar on his face.

I traced his scar with my finger as we lay there next to each other. He couldn't stop staring at me, and I couldn't stop looking at him. Some kind of thread, a magic, was pulling us together, and I didn't want to be away from him now.

"Why do I feel like this? Like it would be painful to separate from you?" I asked. "With my ex-boyfriend, I never felt like this."

"Do you believe in fated mates?" he asked, lifting my hand from his chest and kissing it.

"I mean, not really. It's just something the elders made up in stories," I said.

"Trust me, it's real," he said. "I tried to fight it with you. But it wouldn't let me."

"Why were you trying to fight it?"

"Because my feelings for you scare me. And it would make it much harder to protect you."

Sixteen

LACY

"What do you mean?" I asked, confused about why he was scared to listen to his feelings. I wanted to get to know him more. Figure out his mind and the way he thought before I committed fully.

"Because if you want something, it'll be hard to refuse you," he said gruffly. "Even if it means putting yourself in danger. Your happiness would mean a lot more to me than your safety. And that is a comprising place to be in."

"You're a mysterious alpha," I said, touching his chest as he closed his eyes.

"Oh, what's going on here?" said a male voice at the door. I saw Ethan standing there wide-eyed.

"Shit," I squeaked, scrambling to pull a blanket over me to cover myself, but I was completely knotted to Ryder. His knot was firm, with no signs of letting me go.

"Here," said Ethan, pulling the blanket over us. "Did he somehow lure you to bed, little lass?"

"She lured *me*," protested Ryder. "It started with her panties lying around in my face. Her sweet ginger candy scent called to me."

"My panties weren't lying around like that!" I cried out,

covering my face in embarrassment. "I never planned this would happen. You weren't even supposed to be in my room."

"So you saw her panties and decided to knot her immediately," said Ethan dryly.

"I...yes, Ethan. That is exactly what happened."

"Then what does this mean for our pack?" Ethan asked him, and my pulse raced, scared of his answer. I was scared for him to accept me as his omega and even more scared of his rejection. I wasn't sure what I wanted at all with him.

"It's up to her," said Ryder, locking eyes with me. "It's up to her if she wants to be the omega of our pack or not. What's your answer, Lacy?"

Their eyes were on me.

I gulped. This was a huge commitment, and I was *not* ready. The knot inside me felt so delicious, but I had to be strong. I needed to fight my feelings no matter how comfortable I felt in a long time with an alpha.

"I don't know," I whispered.

"What does that mean?" asked Ryder. "Tell me, Lacy."

"I'm not ready," I said. It surprised me to see Ryder's face fall ever so slightly, and it was awkward saying this while I was knotted to him still. I hated every moment of this. I wanted desperately to have babies and be part of a pack, but I couldn't trust alphas just like that.

"Damn," said Ethan, and my face turned hot.

"May I ask why?" asked Ryder.

"After how my ex-boyfriend treated me, I'm not very trusting of alphas," I said. "I built my career from nothing, and now I don't want to ruin it for anything."

"I understand, but..." said Ryder, touching my face.

"But what?"

"I'll wait until you're ready. Because if it was meant to be, nothing will stop us from being together."

❧

LATER THAT NIGHT, I lay in bed after showering. While in the shower, I couldn't help but think about my first invitation to be an omega for a pack and how open this pack was to me, unlike my ex, who kept me hidden.

I could hear the guards walking around the house late at midnight and settling into their rooms after long naps. The baby shower seemed to have worn out all of us. The cleanup after the baby shower tired me out, but then having mind-blowing sex with Ryder after that took a toll on me.

His words played in my head over and over. *"...nothing will stop us from being together."*

But how did he know if he was ready for an omega? I didn't know anything about *him*, yet I couldn't help but get knotted by him. It was unbelievable to me how strong my desires were when I was around him. After my shower, I still felt his semen leak from my pleasantly sore vagina and his phantom knot inside me. I wasn't a virgin anymore, and I didn't regret that Ryder was my first.

I didn't feel any different after being knotted, but it opened a whole new world.

A strange feeling of emptiness settled within me after I told him my decision. I felt the loneliness deep down to my very being, and I wanted to run back to him. I wanted to confess that I wanted to be his omega and have babies with him. But logically, it didn't make sense to me at all. I closed my eyes, trying to sleep even though my brain was running a mile a minute.

I heard a soft knock at the door, and I pulled the blanket from my hot face.

"Come in," I said. I saw the door opening and the silhouette of Adrian standing there in the shadows.

"Wanna talk?" he said, coming closer to the bed.

"Not really," I said glumly, turning away from him. "I'm exhausted."

"Then allow me to tuck you in."

I felt the bed sink in as he lay down next to me. He silently pulled me in, wrapping an arm around me. Even though my mind screamed at me to kick him out, I felt comfort in his presence. His chest pressed against my back as he spooned me, and the vibrations from him soothed me into a deep sleep.

～

THE FOLLOWING MORNING, my arms were sore from swimming.

As I swam, I thought about everything that happened last night with a fresh, clearer mind. It was all so hazy after our exhausting day. I hadn't seen Ryder yet this morning, and Adrian was still snoring in my bed after spooning me. Cooper greeted me on my way to the swimming pool, warily watching me walk away. I knew he was watching me from the extra cameras they installed.

I was mindlessly swimming, unsure of my life decisions, until I was interrupted by Adrian and Lucas.

"Morning, Lacy," said Lucas. He seemed to be in a chipper mood this morning. "Up early?"

I looked up with water dripping from my face.

"Yep! Morning," I greeted. He jumped into the pool, only wearing shorts, and I groaned internally. It was hard not to feel horny around all these men. But at the same time, having company here would mean I wasn't alone with my thoughts for too long.

"I was worried when I didn't see you next to me," said Adrian, who swam towards me. His hair was already completely wet and plastered to his face.

"Don't worry, I'm still here," I said, lifting my head up for air. I dived deep, swimming for a minute, then paused briefly.

"Yeah, I can see that," he said, floating beside me. "I would just like to know where you go at all times. You could have woken up me- I want to do my job well, you know."

"Since when?" I asked sarcastically. Ever since I met him, he was always joking and playing around.

"Since you," he said, licking his lips as he gazed at me. Tendrils of his long, curly black hair covered his eyes, and he quickly shoved it back. "It may look like I joke a lot, but in reality, my eye was always on you."

My heart beat faster when he looked at me like that. For the first time, he looked like he was being serious.

I was seriously doubting my ability to read people now.

"And I feel the same way," said Lucas, stopping on my other side. My arms were crossed over the pool's edge as I floated between them in the water.

"Lucas, you never even talk to me," I said, shocked.

Did Ryder put them up to this? To butter me up so I could be their pack's omega?

"I'm sorry about that," he said. "I like to keep my professional life separate from my personal life. But now that Ryder has knotted you, that changes things. Doesn't it?"

"What?" I croaked out.

I didn't know what to say when Adrian leaned down to kiss me. His hand wrapped around the back of my neck, pulling me in. His lips were firm against mine, shutting me up effectively. My breathing accelerated at what Lucas said.

They thought I was officially their omega.

And my face heated at the thought of them discussing Ryder knotting me. Or they had all heard my moans from the room while they pretended to sleep downstairs.

I couldn't help but kiss Adrian back. Lucas's arms encircled my waist as he began kissing my neck. Slick seeped between my legs as my pussy clenched hard with these two surrounding me. Walls of muscle around me. Adrian's strong alpha scent washed over me, making me dizzy with desire.

Oh god.

"You smell so delicious," Lucas breathed in my ear. The air from his breath made chills rise on my wet neck. He pressed his full lips against my neck, and I moaned in desire as I felt his warmth seep down my body from his touch.

I felt Lucas's hands roam my ass, grabbing me through my bikini as I kissed Adrian with my eyes closed. I've never felt anything like this. To be sandwiched between two males like this was heavenly to me. It was almost addictive to receive so much sexual attention like this from two powerful males.

"I can't get enough of you. My god," said Adrian against my lips. I smiled shyly as Lucas's kisses on my neck grew more urgent, his hardened dick crushing into my back.

"Me either," I said, not wanting to tell them I rejected Ryder's offer to be their omega.

I just wanted to feel all of this for a few minutes before it all ended, and I told them the truth that I wasn't theirs. Adrian kissed me again, and I felt his hand cup my pussy while Lucas repeatedly squeezed my ass cheeks in his hands.

"Your ass is so cute," mumbled Lucas. "I want to take a bite out of it."

I gasped against Adrian's lips as Lucas dived underwater, and I felt his teeth lightly bite me on my right cheek. My pussy clenched, and Adrian smiled.

"Hmm...your hot pussy is fluttering in my hand," he said, rubbing me over my underwear. His fingers rolled over my clit in circles outside my underwear.

"Please don't tease me like that," I said, trying to hump his hand harder. He smiled, enjoying the control.

"Do you want my fingers inside you, baby girl?" he asked, and my pussy clenched again. Lucas had stopped biting my ass to come up for air, but his hands were still all over my body, touching my thighs and butt. "It shouldn't hurt since Ryder already broke your barrier, didn't he?"

"Did he take your virginity, little omega?" Lucas whispered in my ear, his hot breath searing my skin.

"Yes."

"That turns me on," growled Lucas.

Adrian pulled my panties to the side with his thumb, exposing my pussy.

"What did he do to you?" Adrian asked, rubbing his pointer finger around my clit. I craved for his finger to go deep inside me.

"He knotted me," I panted.

"With what?"

"His cock. Please, Adrian," I gasped when his finger teased my entrance.

"Hmm, I want to finger our omega's ass at the same time," said Lucas.

Seventeen

LACY

My face heated with embarrassment as Lucas ripped my bikini down my thighs, and I kicked it off my feet. They were turning me on like crazy, and I didn't want to stop it. I knew it was wrong to allow them to think I was their omega, but I was fucking horny right now.

My bikini was floating in the water as I felt their fingers feeling me up.

"I can't wait to feel your hot little pussy on my cold finger," said Adrian, teasing me some more as he circled my clit.

"Oh," I gasped when he plunged his finger deep into my slick channel. He grabbed my thigh with one hand, and I wrapped my leg around his waist. "Your finger inside me feels so good."

Then he hooked his finger and started to rub. My pussy clenched at the unfamiliar feeling and invasion. But I was distracted by Lucas spreading my butt cheeks from behind. I was terrified it was going to hurt when he stuck his finger in my behind.

Lucas pressed his thumb around my sphincter. An unfamiliar sensation flowed through me and aroused me like never before.

"I'm going to rub you until you come from your asshole," said Lucas. "Then I'll jam my finger into your tight hole."

Oh my.

"Okay," I whimpered as I felt his thumb circling around and around my anus. Adrian's finger in my pussy rubbed me from the inside until I was shaking with my impending orgasm. I didn't know getting fingered on both ends would feel this good. I never played with my ass the way Lucas was right now, and I loved the feeling.

"Your little ass is getting cleaned right now," said Lucas, rubbing me harder. "Dirty little omegas need to get their asses washed."

The warmth of my slick filled my pussy the more Adrian thrust his finger in and out of my heated core.

I never imagined getting finger-fucked in my swimming pool.

I felt like I was being skewered by their fingers as I floated helplessly in the water between them. My breasts were smooshed to Adrian's chest, and my back was pressed against Lucas's body, his cock dancing in anticipation against my thighs.

"Are you getting every inch of her ass?" asked Adrian, plunging a second finger into my pussy- stretching me even further.

But it was nothing like a knot, so I wasn't too nervous. I pressed my lips on Adrian's shoulder and suddenly had an urge to bite him, but I stopped myself as I screamed through my intense orgasm. I clung to Adrian with shaking legs and arms, leaning on him as Lucas added more pressure to my behind.

His finger swirled around and around. Harder and harder until I cried out.

The warmth of my slick rushed out, and at the same time, Lucas plunged his finger into my asshole. I gasped at the intrusion, closing my eyes and allowing myself to feel it.

"I'm training your bottom for when we knot inside your little ass," said Lucas gruffly, hard at work stretching me. My pussy clenched hard around Adrian's fingers as Lucas played with my butt.

Lucas's finger slid in and out of me gently at first, using the slick I emitted. In and out of my ass until I sighed in contentment.

"Do you like his finger in your ass?" asked Adrian, watching me with lust in his eyes as he slowly unhooked his fingers from my pussy. He lifted his fingers to his face and licked off my juices. "You taste so fucking good."

I blushed. But I couldn't say anything because I was so focused on Lucas's finger in my ass.

"Just like that feels so good," I gasped.

"That's too easy then," said Lucas. "I'm going to stretch you wider, baby."

"No, please!" I said.

But he stuffed a second finger inside of me, and I yelped as he stretched me even more.

The burning feeling slowly disappeared, but I was still nervous about him continuing to stretch me in a place I've never experimented before.

"How are you going to handle our knots then? Your ass needs to be trained."

Just then, I was about to blurt out the real truth about not being their omega. But I looked up to see Ryder and Ethan rushing into the pool room with panicked looks on their faces. Lucas immediately removed his fingers from my behind, and I sighed in relief.

I quickly tried to swim away from Adrian and Lucas, but it was too late. Ryder had seen it all. His eyes roamed to my floating bottoms, and his lips pulled into a smirk.

"Can you grab that for me?" I asked Adrian, and he reached behind him, passing it to me.

"What's going on chief?" Lucas said as he lifted himself out of the pool. His face was cool as a cucumber as he squeezed water from his dark blue shorts, like he wasn't just fingering my ass hole a few moments ago.

"Sorry for disturbing your fun, but she needs to get taken inside immediately," said Ryder.

"Why?" I asked.

"Your stalker is here. We caught him walking around outside through our cameras, and Cooper's after him," said Ethan in a rushed voice. "I'll carry her inside."

I could barely process the information before Ethan lifted me out of the swimming pool with his massive alpha strength. My wet body felt so heavy and tired as he rushed me into the house. My head bounced against his muscled chest as he ran up the steps of my home and into my bathroom.

He deposited me into the tub, and suddenly, I was overcome with giggles.

I couldn't help but laugh as I watched him fumble with the knobs to get the temperature right. He looked so serious in his task.

"What's so funny?" he asked. I covered my mouth, trying to hold back more laughter.

"I mean, the stalker isn't a big deal anymore," I said. "We don't have to be so scared."

"Your safety is a big deal, Lacy," said Ethan, turning on the water.

I didn't even notice when he unclipped my wet top, revealing my breasts to him. I instantly covered myself with my hands when I saw him reaching for the washcloth.

"How about the stalker? Shouldn't you be out there looking for him?"

"My job is to stay with you and protect you," said Ethan, squirting bath soap all over the washcloth until it was covered in pink streaks. "Now relax, omega."

Every limb of my body felt heavy and tired from swimming, so I didn't fight him. I was getting used to these guards feeling me up, and it didn't feel horrible. I just needed to figure out what we would do once my stalker was caught. *Was I going to say farewell to them like nothing happened?*

I felt him rub the washcloth all over my neck and my back.

The warmth of it felt good against my chilled skin. My pussy was still throbbing, and my ass was aching after Lucas's fingers.

I yawned.

A nice nap after this would be nice. Then I remembered we needed to go to the haunted house event of Manny's. Would they stop me from going because of this incident? *They better not stop me.*

"It feels so good," I said to Ethan. I needed him on my side, so I needed to butter him up before the event tonight. "How the heck did you carry me all this way? You're so damn strong."

"Aw, thank you," said Ethan, rubbing the washcloth around my breasts. I could see his face turning red as he did that. "Sorry about this."

"No, it's okay, I'm so worn out. I'd rather you wash me," I said, jutting out my chest so he could see my hard nipples. His face reddened even further as he ran the washcloth over my nipples.

His large, warm hands covering my body felt amazing with every stroke.

He hesitated as he brought the washcloth down to my belly and over my mound. I could see his pants tenting with his arousal as he hesitantly washed the top of my pussy. His Adam's apple bobbed in his throat as he swallowed nervously.

"Spread your legs, my dear," he said. I was getting aroused by this. Even though he was much older than me, it was hot to me.

"Like this?" I asked, spreading my legs wide and lifting them over the edge of the tub in either direction so he could get a good view. I was horny now, so I didn't care as much.

"Oh fuck," he said under his breath. He poured a small bucket of warm water over my pussy, and I jerked at the impact. I was still sensitive from Adrian's fingers thrusting into me wildly. His hand shook as he brought the cloth directly over my pussy. He wiped me with the washcloth in an up-and-down motion. His finger pressed against my center from the washcloth, and I gasped in surprise.

Then he dropped the washcloth to the bottom of the tub and quickly squirted soap over his own hand.

"Umm," I started to say.

"I'll wash you thoroughly, don't worry, little omega," he said.

I bit my lip as he cupped my pussy and rubbed my folds vigorously until it was open for him. Then he stuck his middle finger inside of me, and his thumb rubbed my clit.

Oh god, his feral side was taking over, and I was loving it.

"You do such a good job, Ethan," I moaned, and he pressed his finger harder inside me. Then he removed his finger and picked up the washcloth again. I gasped when he began to stuff the washcloth inside my pussy.

"You're going to be spotless," he growled as we watched half the cloth disappear inside me.

"Oh my goodness," I moaned, enjoying how it filled me up. He slowly pulled it out, and my chest rose and fell in fast breaths.

"Please turn around," he commanded. "I need to wash your butt, little omega."

My heart pounding furiously, I got on all fours, and he washed my butt cheeks in a circular motion with the rag. He squeezed my cheeks unnecessarily with the rag, clapping them together loudly.

"I'm sure Lucas cleaned your ass already, but I'll make sure," he said, spreading my ass cheeks apart with his bare hands.

My face heated.

"So you saw us?"

"I saw every moment he rubbed your anus and how flushed your face got," said Ethan. "I saw the moment he stuck his finger into you, and you jumped."

Then Ethan stuffed his own finger deep into my ass, and I gasped in surprise.

"Oh," I said out loud as he popped his finger out to wash between my cheeks with the rag. He rubbed my anus with it, and I felt the cloth stimulating me.

"Very good," he said, his voice deepening as he watched me

while I was on all fours. I could tell he was getting turned on as much as myself. He moved the rag up and down, washing me thoroughly.

I arched my back, needing more. I wanted more.

Then I felt his bare fingers washing between my ass cheeks, up and down. And every time, he'd stick his finger inside my ass hole, stretching my hole.

"Lucas said he was trying to stretch me before I could take a knot in my ass," I said. "Do you really knot inside the ass?"

"Yes," said Ethan, pressing two fingers into my anus, and I gritted my teeth to get used to being stretched there. "An omega for a pack is used in all ways. Every part of her to satisfy her leader and her pack."

He removed his fingers, and I felt the gush of the water hit my butt as he rinsed me off.

Well, it felt good as hell while it lasted.

Ethan rinsed off my entire body and helped me stand in the tub as he wrapped the towel around me.

"Thank you, Ethan," I said, flashing him a charming smile. A horrifying thought crossed my mind that maybe I was more like my mother than I thought. And that I could be just as manipulative if I wanted to.

Eighteen

LACY

After my bath administered by Ethan, I was busy slathering the scent blocker lotion all over my body while Ethan watched me closely.

He was standing in front of the locked door, and I could tell how horny he was getting as I bent over in my towel, putting lotion on my legs next. The outline of his dick against his pants was prominent.

"What do you think is happening out there?" I asked lightly, making sure my thighs were covered in the cream. I was still highly aroused from the alphas' finger fucking, and I craved something else.

It was impossible to get knotted once and then not crave it again.

Maybe I was turning into some kind of nymphomaniac, and I didn't hate it. Some part of me wished I was in heat so they could all knot me in turn.

"They're taking care of it," he said hoarsely as he watched me. "My job is to stay with you until all is clear."

"Ooh, that's good. I trust you," I said, facing the body-length mirror.

I dropped my towel to the ground and stood there entirely

naked. I could see Ethan in the mirror's reflection, and his pupils darkened as he watched me. His breathing turned harsher as I rubbed the lotion around my medium-sized breasts, making sure to take extra good care of my nipples using my fingers.

"Oh fuck," said Ethan, approaching me. His heavy footsteps sent excitement coursing through my body and slick drenching my pussy. He stopped behind me, pressing me against him. Then he cupped my breasts and squeezed until I cried out. "You're doing this on purpose. You know not to tempt an alpha, yet you do it anyways."

I didn't care. I wanted more.

I needed it.

His rough hands continued to release and squeeze my breasts until he pulled me into a sitting position in front of the mirror. I was sitting between his legs, and then he spread my thighs open with his hands until my pussy was visible.

"What are you doing?" I asked, my voice shaking. I never really looked at myself like that. He spread my legs apart further until I was self-conscious. Thankfully my pussy was shaved today.

"I want to know where I'll knot you," he said huskily. "Go ahead and touch yourself. Spread your lips like how you wanted to in front of me. Don't act shy now."

"No, I was only putting on lotion," I said, suddenly worried. Maybe I shouldn't have gone too far with the teasing. I just needed his support for later. But now I was pretty much stuck doing this, or else he'd lose interest in me.

"Spread those pussy lips," he ordered. "You know better than to tease an alpha locked in a room with you."

With shaking fingers, I dipped my hands down between my legs as we both looked at the mirror. My face was so pink, and my wet hair was plastered down my back. My pussy was already sensitive from all the attention this morning.

"I'm sorry for teasing you," I said. "I didn't mean to."

"Pinch your lips and spread them apart," he said. "Make your alpha happy. It will make me very happy to see your pussy hole. Spread."

I swallowed nervously and used both hands to grab each end of my labia. When I spread my pussy lips open, a small squelching sound emitted from me because of how wet with slick I was. *Oh god.*

"There. Did you have enough now?" I asked, my heart pounding.

"Hold your lips open," he said. "I need to look at your hole. Your pussy is dripping onto your fancy rug, and your pussy is pink, delicious and clenching. Look at that."

"For how long?" I asked, getting more aroused the longer he stared. His eyes bored into the mirror as we both looked at my spread-out pussy. I suddenly longed for something thick to go inside it.

"Just imagine my alpha dick stretching you fully to your heart's desire and pumping all my semen inside you," he whispered, his lips on my damp shoulder. He placed his hand on my stomach. "I would pump into you until your belly is round with my knot. After making sure I impregnate you with my knot, then I would pull out to see your pussy painted in my liquid, soaked and quivering."

My pussy clenched, and we both saw it happen in the mirror. My hands were getting weaker, and I couldn't hold my slippery pussy lips open any longer.

"Oh god," I groaned, wishing just that. His words didn't make it any easier on me. "Why don't you do it then?"

"If I knot you right now and have you writhing under me...I won't be able to protect you now, can I?"

"I don't care," I said, releasing my pussy lips and turning around to face him until I straddled his lap.

I felt his hard cock through his pants, pressing against my pussy and straining to get inside me. He watched me silently as I unzipped his black pants and unbuttoned it. His dick sprung out, released and free. I gasped at the thickness and length of his cock as I wrapped my hand around it.

I could barely grasp it with one hand.

"It could hurt you, my love," he warned, but I adjusted my sitting position so he could slide right inside me. The slickness of my channel made it easy for his dick to make itself at home in my pussy.

"Show me what you can do," I challenged.

He was hesitant at first.

But he immediately grasped my hips and pulled me upwards with the tip of his dick still inside me. The grip from his hands was powerful, and I felt weak as he slammed me down onto his cock, spearing me fully. I moaned out loud at how deep he was inside me. I tried not to scream and draw the attention of the other men even though I wanted to.

He was thick as hell, and to be dropped onto his cock like that so viciously shocked my pussy to surrender.

"That felt good, didn't it?" he asked with one bushy eyebrow raised in question. He was serious when he was ready to rut. There were no jokes or play.

"That...that surprised me," I whispered.

"I'm going to bounce you on my hungry cock," he said with darkened eyes. He lifted me and bounced me repeatedly onto his thick cock. Each bounce stretched my pussy until I almost came. I couldn't believe how intense this older alpha was.

"I thought you were an old-fashioned gentleman," I gasped when he lifted me over his cock for the fourth time. He handled me like I weighed nothing at all. I was just a play toy for him to fuck with.

And I liked it.

"I cannot restrain myself any longer around your mouth-watering scent," he breathed. "Your hot cunt is fully mine at this moment. No one else's."

His hands tightened on my hips, shoving me closer to him until his entire thickness was almost inside me.

"Ah!" I yelped. "You're so big. What the hell?"

"Good, my cock is hungry for you," he said. Then he grasped my ass cheeks and squeezed me harder onto him, sliding the last couple of inches inside me. "Fuck. I'm going to stick my finger into your little asshole. Just pretend another alpha is fucking you from behind."

"Okay," I gasped when he slid his pointer finger into my butt. Then with his other hand, he guided me up and down onto his cock. My thighs strained as I tried to ride him furiously, chasing my own orgasm. His finger in my butt wiggled as I bounced higher and higher onto his rod. "Oh god, it feels..."

I saw stars as I orgasmed around his pulsing dick. My asshole twitched around his finger, and my exhausted pussy clenched as he roared next. His penis swelled, stretching me even further until I panicked. My breaths came out in shallow gasps.

"Don't try to move," he said. "I don't want you getting hurt. Deep breaths, omega. Deep breaths."

I listened, taking deep breaths rapidly as he swelled another inch inside me. This was so intense.

"Can I handle it all?" I asked in a panic when his knot swelled another inch. His cock was buried deep, and the swelling was happening at the base of his member. His hot liquid streamed inside me, none of his liquid escaping me.

"You can," he said. Then, sensing my panic, he pulled me to him in a hug and purred into my neck and ear. His rumbling chest communicated calmness to me, calming my inner omega wolf. My pussy naturally stretched more, allowing his knot to ease inside me. "You're an omega, my love, and I hadn't mated one in a long time. The betas cannot handle me."

"Oh?" I said with my head against his chest as we sat like that on the ground, my legs spread-eagled around his waist while his knot was inside me. "How long haven't you had sex for?"

"With age, it gets harder for an alpha to find a mate. His knot gets bigger and more intense," he explained. "Omegas are usually terrified, so it's been ten years."

"If I knew that…" I said.

"Then you wouldn't have hopped onto my lap," he said. "There, I'm fully knotted inside you. I presume you're taking heat suppressants, correct? I know that you were hesitant about being our omega."

"I'm just scared my career will be over," I explained, enjoying how his chest rumbled whenever he talked. I rubbed his chest under his dress shirt, admiring his well-built body. It's been so long since I was around males, and I was getting more addicted to the knot every day.

"Your career would flourish," said Ethan. "With our support and love. It's not like we'd throw all the babies to you to take care of. We would all help out because we are one big pack unit."

The door suddenly opened, and with my heart pounding, I looked up.

It was Ryder, and he was looking at us with shock. This was the second freaking time he caught me being intimate with one of his men. He must be thinking that I was some kind of whore.

"Ah, Ethan, I never expected you to…well, never mind on that," he said slowly, watching us as I turned red. "The coast is clear, and we were unable to capture the stalker."

"We need to catch the fucker," said Ethan. "I'll come out there in a few. As you can see, I'm trying to bask in the after-knot moment."

"Can't believe you knotted her."

"She hopped onto my lap," said Ethan. "Who am I to refuse *that*?"

They were discussing me like I wasn't there, and my face burned bright.

"Okay, stop," I said in a low voice. "It's none of your business, Ryder."

"It's fully my business if you decide to fuck my pack," said Ryder. "Your baby will be our responsibility. Your safety, your soul, and your heart would be ours to protect. All of you is my business."

Nineteen

LACY

Later that day, after being knotted by Ethan, he and Ryder were reviewing the cameras while I cooked lunch with Adrian.

"Have you ever made spaghetti before?" I asked Adrian.

He had dumped the uncooked pasta into the water before the water boiled, and I watched with amusement as he looked at the pasta, confused.

I had decided to make lunch for the pack before telling Ryder that I wanted to go to the haunted house event. If I could get the pack obsessed with me, I was sure it would help. And It would mean a lot to Manny if I showed up. I wanted to be the supportive, cool aunt and couldn't bear disappointing him, especially since he had a rough childhood and was made fun of in school for having fathers who were sigmas. And I think it would be fun to scream and squeal in a haunted house with everyone.

"Nope, what's wrong with it?" he asked, looking at me as he leaned against the counter.

"You're supposed to wait until the water boils," I said.

"Whoops, sorry about that," he said, rubbing his hand over my ass as I scowled at the lukewarm pot. I slapped his hand away, and he grinned. "You won't slap me away once you're in heat, baby."

"What makes you think I'll ever go into heat?" I asked, throwing the diced tomatoes into the saucepan with the onions. The truth was, ever since I got knotted twice - I envisioned how it would feel to be knotted constantly. Because I never imagined how good it would feel to be knotted, not even being in heat. I would never stop my heat suppressants just like that. And it just wasn't going to happen.

"You never know," he said. "One of us could easily switch out your pill bottle. It's your duty to have our babies when we want them."

"Psh, that's in the old days," I sighed, rolling my eyes as I mixed the pot.

Then Lucas joined us in the kitchen, backing up Adrian on his stance.

"I believe omegas should be impregnated," he said. "Modern days make it too easy for an omega."

"What?" I said, shocked, almost dropping the mixing spoon. "You can't really believe that."

"Our kind would die out if that doesn't happen," said Lucas. "Why wouldn't you want a baby?"

Shit. I must have hit a sore spot by saying it out loud. I had to let them know I wasn't really their omega, but first, I needed to ask Ryder about the haunted house situation.

"I mean...I might consider it one day," I said.

He seemed happy with that answer, and once we all settled down at the table for lunch, I kept the conversation light as we all ate, and Ryder seemed to be in a good mood. Ethan looked like he was on a high after knotting me, and he was all smiles every time our hands brushed when I passed him utensils or the salt. The pack was cheerful, and I was glad my chances of getting what I wanted would be higher.

After lunch, Ethan and Lucas volunteered to take care of the dishes and told me to relax. So I decided to start getting ready for the event, but before I reached my room, I heard the piano playing from my nest room.

Confused, I walked into the room to see Cooper sitting at the piano playing a beautiful melody to the song 'Moon Bright' amidst the mess from all the feathers. My heart beat faster in my chest as I walked towards him. I couldn't believe this delta played music and he never told me. His face was enraptured in the beauty of the song that his slim hands created on the keys. I sat beside him on the bench and let the music flow through me.

I wanted to join him in the language that was music.

My voice rang in the room in a light lilt, letting the song fly from my soul while he played the piano. I could feel the rest of the pack crowd into the room, watching as he played the piano. Time stood still when he pressed the last key, the sound echoing through the room.

We sat for a moment, looking at each other while the men clapped behind us.

"Man, what the fuck Cooper?" said Adrian, clapping his packmate on the back.

"I didn't know you could play," said Ryder, shaking his head. Cooper was smiling, his face red from all the praises.

"Thanks guys," he said.

I was equally as shocked, and when the men left the room, I looked at him with my eyebrows raised.

"What was that about? Why didn't you tell me you played music, too?"

"I don't like talking about it," said Cooper. "My family doesn't like it and said I'd embarrass the entire community of deltas if they knew about it."

I couldn't imagine hiding my talent away.

"You're really good," I said. When I said that, the joy in his eyes told me that he hadn't heard that often about himself. "Hasn't anyone ever told you that?"

"You're the first," he said, looking at me with a newfound expression. I wasn't prepared when his hand slid across the piano to grab my waiting one on the bench. His massive hand encircled mine as he gazed at me, and I couldn't break the eye contact either.

It was all too consuming. Too intense.

I couldn't believe I was feeling this way about all the guards here. His ice-blue eyes made my heart beat out of my chest. And when he pulled me closer, he gently kissed me on the lips. It all happened in a split second.

"Sorry," he said hastily, getting up from the bench. I didn't get a chance to say anything before he quickly exited the room.

I sat there with my heart beating so fast it was ridiculous.

I placed a finger over my lips, tracing the outline that his cool lips had left. I craved more of him, but leading them on would be dangerous. These men were growing real feelings for me.

After I asked about the haunted house, I'd have to let them all know that all the feelings were over, and my heart sank at the thought. It would be the hardest thing I ever did, but it must be done. I couldn't lead the pack on anymore, even though I enjoyed this attention more than I wanted to.

∼

AFTER GETTING ready to go to the event, I looked at myself in the mirror.

The black catsuit was perfect. Everyone would be dressed up in different costumes tonight. My costume was sexy, clung to my skin, and my bodyguards wouldn't be able to resist my request tonight. Tonight, I wanted to have fun this time instead of working. I touched the fake tail, loving the feel of the sleek fake fur. My headband with the little ears was so cute with my high ponytail.

I smeared on dark, sultry lipstick and purple eyeshadow to go with my look. I knew Olivia was wearing something similar but as an orange cat instead. I had no idea how the bodyguards would react to me. I was slightly apprehensive and scared, but I forced my feet out of my room.

As I walked down the stairs, I saw the men talking amongst each other as they watched the cameras intensely, looking like they had discovered something. They didn't even notice when I appeared in the living room.

"Hey guys," I said, leaning against the stairwell in my heels seductively. When their gaze landed on me, my face burned. All of them had the same hungry look in their eyes. The look of desire and longing that I so enjoyed more than I wanted to. My heart was beating so freaking hard as they stared.

"Hello there, sexy," said Ethan.

"Damn," whistled Adrian.

Ryder didn't say anything. He simply watched me with lifted eyebrows. He looked wary and on guard of what I was going to say. Damn it, that was a bad sign. I needed him to be happy and on board. I've tried everything today to have him in good spirits. Two of the males had gotten to knot me and were well-fed now.

But at least I'd have the support from all the men if I asked.

I had planned this perfectly.

"What are you guys doing?" I asked, sauntering to them with my cat's tail swishing behind my ass. The suit was made out of spandex and was hot against my skin, but it also made me feel incredibly sexy. Every move I made turned me on more than it turned on the bodyguards.

"We're just reviewing the cameras," breathed Cooper.

I noticed Lucas checking out my ass the entire time, and my pussy twitched at the intense look he was giving me. He looked completely enraptured and it made me blush even harder.

"What's the occasion?" coughed Ryder, who looked away and focused on his laptop instead. My heart was beating so fast I thought I might pass out. He looked like he didn't even want to hear it. But I had to be brave.

"Maybe the kitty's in heat," said Lucas, his voice gruff with arousal. His pants were tented and ready to rut me if the need arose.

My pussy responded equally in need when I saw his erection.

My inner omega wolf wanted him, succeeding in turning on these men.

Well, now I had all these men at my fingertips. If I acted sad enough at Ryder's rejection of my request, they'd all feel so sorry for me.

"Ryder, do you remember when I was invited to the haunted house event at the palace?" I said. "I'm still planning on going if you don't mind guarding me today."

"Ooh," said Adrian, his eyes lighting up.

Ryder looked up at me with a serious expression.

"I'm sorry, Lacy, but after everything that's happened," said Ryder. "It can't happen today. He was just here."

"Do you want me to stay cooped up forever in my home?" I asked, batting my eyelashes.

"Ryder, have some compassion," said Ethan gruffly. The other men's faces had softened, watching me pout. I was upset, but it wasn't worse than when I had to skip my singing gig.

"It's not that," sighed Ryder, shutting his laptop. "I don't want you to get hurt. After tonight, I promise this won't happen."

"But aren't you supposed to guard and not trap me?"

"That's true, but..."

"Ryder, just let her," said Adrian. "Look how prettily she dressed up to go."

"I feel bad, man," said Lucas.

"Final answer is no," said Ryder sharply, and I bit my lip. It was all too much now. I couldn't play by his rules anymore.

"That's okay then," I said in a chipper voice so they didn't think I was sad. "I'll go take a nap then."

I headed upstairs to my room, my heart pounding hard. I was ready with a backup plan anyway and definitely not about to nap.

Twenty

LACY

Opening the window in my room, I looked out to see a smiling Olivia waving at me from the grass. The tall ladder she set up for me was leaning against the wall, and I could see her furry orange tail as she shuffled her feet in excitement. I locked my room just in case any of the men decided to come in.

I talked with Olivia a few days after Ryder stopped me from attending my singing gig. I was determined not to be trapped forever in my home, and Olivia was always there when I needed her.

Lifting the meshed net out of the window, I gently set it on my chair. Then I lifted my leg over the window sill and felt for the ladder with my toe while I held my heels in my hand. There wasn't a camera on this side of the house since I told the men I needed privacy in my room. But it came in handy since I needed an escape plan like this.

My legs shook with each step down the ladder.

When I reached the last step, I breathed a sigh of relief when my bare feet finally touched the grass. The straps of my heels were wrapped around my wrist, and I quickly put them on, stumbling on the grass and scared to death that the bodyguards would discover I was gone.

All my bravery was shot out the window now.

"Girl, how could they lock you up in there?" asked Olivia.

"He wouldn't say yes," I said. "I tried everything."

"Did you even try to seduce them? You're so bad at it," she said, laughing.

"No wonder I was a virgin until now," I muttered as I finished strapping my heels. We started walking toward her car after we opened the little door attached to the front gate.

"What do you mean *until now*?" asked Olivia wide-eyed.

"I'll tell you once we get into the car," I whispered, looking around. I was scared the guards would hear me with their sensitive alpha hearing. I had no idea what would happen if they knew I left. The worst that could happen was that they would quit on me, and I was fine with that as long as I had my freedom. But I knew deep down I would miss the attention they each gave me in their different ways.

"Okay, you better tell me now," said Olivia once we were in her car and the doors were shut. I took in a long breath, unsure whether to tell her or not.

"I can't. It's so unprofessional what we did," I said.

She tapped her long, red-painted fingernails against the steering wheel. "You better tell me. Was it a group thing? Did you get knotted?"

"No, it wasn't like that," I said, laughing. "Fine, I had sex with the leader and...his right-hand alpha."

"Oh my god," she said in stunned silence, and I couldn't help smiling. "You're not a virgin anymore. How the hell does a knot feel? Does it hurt?"

Olivia was an omega like myself and wasn't mated to an alpha pack. The one thing we had in common was no contact with alphas' knots unless we were serious about them.

"It's scary at first," I said, trying to explain it right so she didn't get freaked out for her first time. "But you'll get used to it and crave it more."

"Wow," she said as she turned right on the street. "My pussy hurts just thinking about it."

"Yeah," I said. "But I don't want to be tied down to a pack yet. I'm at the height of my career."

"You need to listen to what your body needs, though," said Olivia.

"Nope," I said.

"You're going to get old and un-stretchable."

"I don't care," I said, and it was her turn to laugh. I started to feel guilty, like a teenager sneaking out of her parents' home. Then, I looked out the window as we neared the palace. "Damn, that haunted house looks fancy as hell."

"Wow, Manny put in some work," she said, admiring the grand house painted in black and grey. It looked like a dilapidated mansion. "I'm already fucking scared."

∼

WHEN OLIVIA and I approached the haunted house, we greeted Manny, who was eagerly waiting outside the house next to his mother, Princess Lyra, who was ushering in guests of the palace who wanted to check it out.

"So cool you guys are here," said Manny, hugging both of us. His long black hair was tied into a bun, and he wore a checkered blue shirt with black jeans. He didn't care much about his appearance and didn't present as an alpha yet. People suspected he might present to be a sigma like his fathers. I wasn't worried about that at all, I just wanted him to be happy, but society wouldn't simply accept him into the community if he was a sigma.

"We're here!" I said, hugging him back. My brother Gabe showed up out of nowhere with a bright smile. He loved hanging at the palace even though my mother hated to come here, a reminder of her past faults.

"How are you, Olivia?" asked Manny. While he and Olivia talked, I turned to my brother.

"How's Mom doing?" I asked him.

"Mom already misses you despite the vacation you took with us," he said, rolling his eyes.

"Aww," I said. "We need to go on another vacation soon. Did you see the inside of the haunted house yet?"

"I've seen it a million times already," he said. "You're going to get so scared."

"No, I'm not."

"Yes, you will. You can't handle scary."

"Alright, who's ready to go inside the haunted house with me?" announced Manny, interrupting our sibling argument, even though we were in our twenties. Our fights would sometimes get so bad we wouldn't talk to each other for days.

We all walked inside, with Manny leading the way in. I was the last one in the line, and I couldn't help but shuffle behind Olivia. She was already screaming when we were shrouded in complete darkness.

"I want to leave," she whined when we came upon a dimly lit piano with a skeleton lying on top of it. It was covered in cobwebs, and the haunted house gave off a creepy olden-days vibe.

"We can't leave already," I said. But I screamed when I saw a man wielding an axe in the corner. "Okay, never mind. It's scary as fuck."

I could hear the boys laughing at the front as Olivia, and I screamed like madwomen. Then, we suddenly reached a dark maze, and the dimming of the lights completely disoriented me. I heard Olivia screaming again, but this time it sounded muffled like she was way ahead of me.

Oh fuck. We were completely separated now.

How the hell did I lose her? Stay calm.

As I walked into the labyrinth of glass mirrors- it all lit up around me. There were dark patches between the mirrors, where the monsters would pop out of. I hugged myself as I passed by them, constantly screaming.

I had to get the fuck out of here. I couldn't scream for the others, or the costumed monsters would notice my fear and scare me even more. I hoped to sneak up on them so they wouldn't have time to scare me.

But when I passed by a particular shadow, I screamed when he grabbed me around the waist. I was breathing hard when he pulled me close and covered my mouth with a gloved hand.

Oh my god. This couldn't be happening right now.

The monsters weren't supposed to touch me, so I was confused. And I hoped it wasn't my worst fear coming to life.

"Hi, Pinkie," he growled in a low voice.

My fear had just turned into a real fright for my life.

It was him.

I froze. His other hand roamed over my belly as he breathed hard. I felt his dick pressing into my behind as I felt his arousal. His scent was like an alpha's, but it was familiar. I couldn't point it out.

"One day, I'm going to breed you," he said, rubbing my belly. "I'm coming for you soon, baby. It's almost time for your season."

When he suddenly released me, I dashed away from him. I started running for my life while crashing into mirrors. I screamed and yelled for help as I ran away helplessly. And as I ran, I looked back to see his shadow chasing me around.

∽

Ryder

I FELT terrible as I stared at my screen, replaying the footage.

Lacy was actually listening to my orders, and that somehow made me feel worse. I thought she would have thrown another tantrum until, eventually, I'd give in. I was a lot weaker to her charms now than she thought.

But I couldn't let her know that.

"I think we should just go with her there," said Lucas, sensing my uncertainty. I slammed my laptop closed once again.

"You might be right," I sighed. "I feel fucking weird about it. I'm going to check on her and see if she still wants to go."

"Finally, he comes to his senses," mumbled Adrian.

As I walked up the stairs, my pack followed behind me, eager to get another glimpse of the omega. I didn't have the heart to tell them she didn't want us as a pack. Only Ethan knew that, yet he still knotted the fuck out of her today. He was probably scared he wouldn't get another chance at omega pussy, and I didn't blame him. I was getting excited as I prepared to tell her we would go to her dreadful event together.

I gently knocked on her door twice. No answer.

"She's probably sleeping," said Ethan, disappointed.

"Hmm," I said, standing at her door. I felt a breeze hit me from below her door onto my ankles. "Her window's open."

"So?" said Cooper.

"Since I've been here, I've never seen her open the window," I muttered. I knocked harder on her door and didn't get a response. "Lacy! If you're in there, open the door or say something to me."

Nothing.

Shit. That wasn't a good sign.

I kicked the door, and it slammed open, bouncing off the wall in my rage. I scanned the room, and there was no sign of her anywhere.

"She's not in the bathroom," said Lucas darkly.

I ran to her window, seeing the ladder positioned perfectly under her window.

"Fuck!"

Twenty-One

LACY

"Pinkieeee! Pinkieee!"

His voice reverberated around the maze as I huddled in a corner, eyes shut and holding my ears. *Please go away. Please go away.* His voice mingled with groaning from the other monsters and the whirring fog machine.

Only I could hear his voice.

The nightmare that was only mine.

"Stop it!" I screamed with my eyes shut. I had to find my way out of this mess, but the more I ran, the more lost I became.

I tried to drown out his chants by humming to myself.

Maybe if I stayed behind long enough, my brother would get worried and return for me. Or he was probably getting a good laugh out of me taking so long in this maze. I should never have come here.

Suddenly, I felt hands grab my upper arms. I screamed bloody murder.

"Stop, let me go!" I screamed endlessly. I was wheezing and out of breath.

It was too early for me to die. My family would miss me.

"Shh, Lacy," he said, shaking me. I didn't want to open my

121

eyes to see the monster before me. The stalker who wanted to breed me with his spawn. "Open your eyes. It's me, Ryder!"

His last command was a bark.

I opened my eyes, and relief flowed through me, seeing his bald head under the reflecting lights. His scar was no longer intimidating but comforting. I threw myself at him, grabbing him tight.

"He's here," I gasped out. "Do you hear him?"

"What? Who's here?"

"The stalker. He's in here."

But the chanting stopped. The nickname the stalker thought up for me ringing through the maze of mirrors stopped.

It was silent, except for the groans of the monsters.

"I don't see him," said Ryder, looking around cautiously. Then his eyes darkened when he turned his gaze back to me. "We have a lot to talk about. You shouldn't have left the house alone, do you understand?"

"I'm sorry," I said, but he was silent as he helped me get to my feet. Cooper had come up behind me, with Lucas and Adrian flanking either side. I grabbed a hand on each side of me, feeling safer now that they were here.

Apprehension settled inside me as I followed Ryder out of the maze. His stony demeanor showed that he wasn't happy with me at this moment.

My stomach tightened with apprehension.

~

WHEN WE RETURNED to my house, I collapsed onto the couch, and Adrian helped me unstrap my heels.

Ryder was pacing around the living room, his face tense.

I didn't dare ask him what he was thinking about. I knew I messed up big time with how deep in thought he was. He was probably thinking of ways of how to handle me.

"Lacy," said Ryder in a heavy voice as he sat beside me. Adrian finished removing my heels and rubbed my ankle comfortingly before walking away.

"Yes?"

"Why did you sneak out?" he asked, crossing his fingers on his lap.

"I just wanted to have some fun," I said. "Listen, you're not my dad or anything. Whatever happened is past. I apologize for it, and now let's move on."

I was tired of him putting me on edge and making me feel bad the entire ride home. It was all my choosing if I wanted to put myself in danger.

It had nothing to do with him at all.

"You don't sound too apologetic," he said. He looked at me with something feral in his eyes, and I grew uneasy. He grasped my wrist, and I froze, watching him to see what he planned to do. "I may have to discipline you, omega."

"But I'm not your mate," I said. "And I'm damn well glad that I'm not!"

"What?" said Lucas in surprise. "I thought she was our omega."

Oh shit.

"She chose not to," said Ryder, dragging my unwilling body onto his lap. I squirmed and kicked until he had me face down on his lap. My face was pressed against the pillows of the couch, and my ass was on his lap. He rubbed his hand over my ass, which was covered in the spandex material. "And she tricked you all into thinking that she was."

"What the hell are you doing?!" I shouted, trying to wriggle away, but he firmly grasped my thighs. I twisted around to punch him, but Ethan held my forearms still.

They were helping him. They knew I wasn't their omega now.

"You put yourself in danger," said Ryder. "Against alpha's orders."

He unzipped the back of my suit, and I felt it loosen around me. The cold air hit my sweaty skin when the material exposed my ass. My pussy clenched at the worst time ever. Fuck, I was getting horny again from his touch. I had to try and control it, but when I felt slick drip down my thighs - I knew it was too late.

I wanted to feel every spank.

"I'm pretty sure this is not in your bodyguard handbook," I said breathlessly. He slowly rubbed his palm against my ass cheek in preparation. "I promise it won't happen again."

∾

Ryder

"I'll make sure you mean that promise," I growled, rubbing her ass threateningly.

I couldn't take chances with this omega. She was a naughty one who'd never been disciplined in her life. It would hurt me to discipline my client.

But it needed to be done.

Earlier, when I found her room empty, my heart had dropped. I felt like I had failed if anything happened to her.

Her ass wiggled and squirmed on my lap, releasing her scent of arousal in the air.

"I'm sorry, Lacy," I said in a low voice. My cock hardened under her as her scent wafted to my nose. Fuck, I couldn't get enough of her smell. Tonight, I would hunt for her panties once she discarded them in the basket. "This will ensure that it doesn't happen again."

"Why?"

"It's either we walk out and give up guarding you, or you will accept the spanking I'm about to give you."

She hesitated.

Her round ass underneath my palm was warm, jiggling at the

slightest touch. She was ready to be spanked, whether or not she liked it. But I would give her the choice now.

"I can take the spanking," she said, and I raised my eyebrows. She was trying to show a brave face.

"Be easy on her," said Ethan, still holding her arms.

"Ryder, do you really have to?" said Adrian, standing defensively at her head like a guard dog. Lucas watched from the other couch, his dick standing straight up inside his pants. Cooper was outside doing who-knows-what.

"She must learn a lesson," I muttered, rubbing her right ass cheek first. I pulled her panties down, seeing them already sticky with her slick when I revealed the inside of it. Clear slick coated every inch of her panties as I pulled it down her thighs. Her ass was now fully exposed, the globes of her cheeks sitting firm.

I brought my palm down on her ass, and she jerked over my hard cock. I loved how her ass cheek turned pink so fast.

Smack. The sound of her yelp turned me on even more.

The second smack came down.

Her ass jiggled, and I couldn't help but dip my face down to smell her pussy. Her pussy smelled so good with each spank.

"Are you...are you done?" she whispered in a shaky voice.

"Have you learned your lesson yet?" I growled, licking her pussy, and she trembled on my lap. Her fear and arousal were turning me on so much I was about ready to rut her to kingdom come.

"No," she said.

"That's what I thought," I said, smacking her again across both her ass cheeks. Her ass jiggled and shook even more. I looked at her pussy again and saw more slick bubbling inside her pussy ready to drip out. She was getting horny with every smack. She was supposed to learn a lesson.

She wasn't supposed to get off on it.

This time I smacked her harder across her ass, my palm glancing over her pussy so she felt it. This time, she yelped and squirmed.

Good. That was what I needed to see. A little healthy fear was always good. I spanked her again in the same spot, and she yelled at me this time.

"Okay! That's enough," she screamed. But I bent my head again to peek, and I saw that her pussy was now dripping onto my thighs. I needed her wide open and spread now.

I flipped her over until her head was hanging off the couch, and her thighs were open on my lap. So I had a direct view of her entire pussy.

"Much better," I said, spreading her thighs apart before me while she was upside down, with Ethan managing to steady her.

"Oh my god, you're crazy," she gasped, trying to kick me in the face, but I held her still. With her legs spread wide open, I squeezed her ass cheeks and saw more slick coat her little pussy. The musky scent of her sweat filled my nose when I bent my head down. I licked her pussy again, and she moaned, her toes curling. I swiped my thick tongue over her pulsing clitoris and pressed my nose into her pussy.

She smelled so fucking good.

But I had a job to finish. I flipped her back to the original position with her ass on my lap to spank her. I brought my hand down onto her ass, three more times on each cheek, until she cried out for me to stop. I was breathing just as hard as her, my balls tight as fuck. I wanted to fucking knot her.

As I gazed at her, her blushing bottom looked so cute, like a tomato.

"Did you learn your lesson?" I asked again.

"Yes," she gasped. "Please, no more."

Feeling bad that she was probably hurting, I grabbed the ice pack Lucas handed me. It was an ice cube wrapped in a paper towel, and I held it her ass until the tension in her body eased.

"You're not going to run away again. Do you hear me, omega?"

She hesitated to answer me right away. Fuck, she was such a stubborn one.

"I understand," she said in a short voice.

As I rubbed the ice over her, I enjoyed how her burning ass felt against my palms. She was finally going to listen and not put herself in danger again. Her reckless behavior nearly got her killed. When I found her crying in the maze, I wanted to strangle the motherfucker who scared her.

It shouldn't happen again.

Twenty-Two

LACY

I felt humiliated and embarrassed.

I didn't say a word when Ethan helped me stand back up on shaky legs. I pulled my panties back up over my thighs that Ryder had ripped off. I groaned in pain when the fabric touched my burning ass, so I pulled it off and stomped upstairs with it in my hands.

"Save those panties aside for me," growled Ryder, and I ignored him, but my pussy twitched in response.

"Don't follow me," I hissed at the guys.

None of them stopped Ryder from delivering his archaic punishment. And he had the honor of licking my pussy too. I was still throbbing with arousal, and my stomach clenched for an orgasm, but I didn't dare beg him for that. I couldn't show any weakness in front of them.

I locked the bathroom door and sat on the toilet. Sitting on there for a little while would be easier than sitting directly on a chair. My ass burned, but it wasn't too bad after the ice he applied to it. Familiar rage began brewing inside of me. Tears pricked my eyes and flowed down my face.

I cried, with my face buried in my hands. I lost all track of time when I was done.

128

Then I got up and wrapped myself in a bath towel. I should probably shower, but when I looked at myself in the mirror, I saw someone I didn't want to be reminded of—the broken girl years ago who was kicked out into the rain by her ex. My makeup was smeared from my crying, returning me to those terrible memories. All these years of building my life and self-esteem were destroyed in one moment.

There was no way I was going to let it happen again.

With rage simmering inside me, I burst out of the bathroom and stomped back down the stairs with tears streaming down my face- my towel still wrapped around my body. The men stopped talking and looked at me with widened eyes.

"Out! All of you!" I screamed. I saw nothing but red right now.

"What are you saying?" asked Ryder slowly as he got up from the couch. Ready to walk over to me and threaten me again.

Like hell, he would.

"You're fucking fired," I shouted. "Get out of my house. No one ever lays a finger on me like that, and this will be the last time it ever happens. I never want to see your faces again."

"Are you sure, Lacy?"

"I'm damn sure," I said, seething internally.

"If that's what you want, then," said Ryder, stony-faced. He nodded to his team. "Get all your things."

"Lacy, we're sorry," said Adrian, his eyes flicking between me and Ryder. There was nothing but tension between us, and my heart raced with rage and adrenaline.

"I spent years building myself up," I said. "I'm not about to let all of you ruin it for me. None of you defended me when Ryder went crazy on me. None of you helped me when I wanted to leave the house to have some fun or even go to work."

The men looked morose and upset as they gathered their weapons, hiding in every crevice of my house. I gripped my towel tightly to my chest as I watched them. The air conditioner dried the tears on my cheeks while I stood there like a statue at the bottom of the staircase.

Adrian and Cooper tried talking to me, but I wasn't having it.

I didn't want to hear from any of them. The heartbreak on the men's faces was evident when they finally knew I wasn't their omega and that there would never be a chance of us happening. When they were finally leaving, Ryder looked back at me again at the front door.

"It was great knowing you, Lacy," he said. "I'm sorry if I scared you. Don't be reckless, and take care of yourself. Okay?"

Something about him standing there, looking at me with sadness in his eyes, made me want to bawl and cry. But I held myself together.

Be strong, Lacy.

"Have a good night," I said. He gave me one last lingering look, and I closed the door behind him. Taking a deep breath, I looked up at the ceiling and saw that all the cameras they had installed were gone. Good riddance.

But as I walked up the stairs, I was crying again. *Damn, these tears.* I hadn't cried like this in such a long time, and it was ridiculous. The house suddenly felt barren, empty, and quiet when the armored car zoomed off. Once I was in my room, I grabbed my phone and dialed Olivia's number.

After I told her what happened, I needed her to tell me I was being stupid for feeling this way. I really needed her support right about now. But the phone rang and rang- so I ended the call, sighing.

I felt uneasy, and something was nagging at me, but I couldn't place it.

∿

I WAS SLEEPING PEACEFULLY until I woke up to a hand gripping my waist.

My eyes flew open, and I saw a hulking figure standing over

me in the darkness of my room with his hand on my waist. I tried to scream, but there was a cloth wrapped around my mouth. Heart-pounding wildly, I reached out to push him away, but my hands were tied behind my back.

"Settle down, pinkie," he said, his voice muffled with a mask.

No. No. No.

I thought I had locked all the doors. I even double-checked before going to bed.

Heart racing within my chest, he lifted me effortlessly over his shoulder like I was a bag of potatoes. I tried to kick and squirm out of his grasp, but it was useless. He carried me down the stairs like I weighed nothing at all.

"You shouldn't have left that ladder at your window," he said, chuckling, and I groaned at how dimwitted I was. First, I leave the ladder for easy access and then fire the only bodyguards willing to put up with me.

I was basically a sitting duck.

I tried to scream even with the rag wrapped around my mouth, just in case anyone could hear my muffled yells. I looked up and saw that he was walking towards a black car with tinted windows. Sunrise was starting to show, and I realized it was already the next morning. When I head butt his ear, he didn't budge an inch. I knew it had to hurt him even a little because my own head was hurting.

He dumped me into the car and sat beside me in the backseat.

"You finally have her," said the scratchy voice of the driver.

"It took fucking forever, but the famous omega singer is here now," said my stalker.

I stared at him with narrowed eyes as I scooted to the other end of the seat until my body was pressed up the door. I needed to put as much space between us as possible. I didn't want to be near the man who terrorized me for the last few days. My hands were still tied behind my back, and I tried to wiggle my wrists, but the bonds were secure.

The stalker ripped off his mask, and that's when I got a good look at his face. And my heart dropped.

It was my ex-boyfriend, Jordan.

He smiled wildly, seeing the look of shock in my eyes. He leaned over, untying the cloth around my mouth. Even with it off, I was speechless. Why the hell was he doing this? I never thought he would be capable of this at all.

"Why?" I croaked. Sleep was still in my voice, and I felt like I was in some sort of nightmare. I hoped to god this *was* just a nightmare.

He sighed, crossing his arms behind his neck as he looked towards the front.

"I decided I needed to change my life," he said. "I wanted to make a difference in this world by taking omegas to a special camp. Especially you."

"What camp are you talking about? Are you okay, Jordan?"

"I'm more than okay," he snapped, lowering his arms and looking at me with darkened eyes. "I never take disrespect from omegas anymore. Omegas are difficult now because they are free to mate whatever degenerate crosses their path. Betas, Deltas, Sigmas, and now fucking vampires. It's not the natural order of how it should happen."

I wondered how I never saw a warning sign that this guy was a weirdo. I never imagined in a million years Jordan would do this.

"So what if omegas mate them?" I said.

"Then alphas will be extinct," he answered. "Omegas need to bear the children from alphas. They are made for alphas and no one else."

"Why do you even care, Jordan?" I asked, trying to reason with him as the car drove further away from my home. The sun was now fully up and shining brightly down my face that I could barely see him.

His face looked tired, and his blond hair was unkempt.

His jeans were torn in several places. He looked worse for wear after I hadn't seen him for five years. I remembered how he took

CRAVED BY THE PACK

care of himself in the past and even trimmed his nails, but now he looked like he didn't care.

"When you rejected me, I knew that was it," said Jordan, scratching his unkempt beard. "You were the sixth omega who didn't care to be knotted by me. How do you think I felt after being rejected and led on for months by you? And yet, you allow a delta to tickle your butt and multiple alphas to knot you. Yes, I watched it all."

My face twisted in disgust at that moment. He was lost in his thoughts as he looked out the window. He was sick in the head for spying on me, and I suddenly realized how dangerous my situation was.

"I just wasn't ready. I was young," I explained.

"That's what they all say," he spat out. "You were the last straw. So, I joined the organization that would bring omegas under control again. An organization that hates the government for allowing vampires to live amongst us and take our omegas."

"What do you want with me?"

"To breed you," he said with an evil smile. "We will create babies with you. To produce more alpha werewolves and to prevent the extinction of our kind."

Twenty-Three

LACY

"What the hell?" I said.

I was at a complete loss of what to say. He was much crazier than I thought, and he hid it well. Now I knew why the stalker's scent was familiar to me.

"You'll be taught to serve your alphas," he said.

I was trembling with panic, flashes of my family going through my mind. All they would see was my name on the news. Another omega that had gone missing.

"Is that where the omegas have gone missing? Like on the news?" I asked while I secretly tried to loosen the ropes around my wrists, but it was futile.

"Some yes," he said. "They've gone to a better place. They know their place now as the omega of their pack."

He was absolutely nuts.

I had no idea where we were going now. The roads were long and winding down, getting sandier the farther out we went. The island was so big that a whole side could even be uninhabited. My mouth was dry, and I was still wearing my silk pink pajamas dotted with tiny white flowers.

"Why me?" I asked him after a long pause.

"You're the most successful omega on Howl's Edge right now.

All eyes will be on the news when they report you missing, and the government will know we're serious," he said. "My job is to recruit omegas to the Omega Breeding Camp, or the OBC as we call it. You're going to be the best catch of all. I might even get a pay raise, so Henry better pay up."

I didn't know whether to feel flattered or sick.

Not wanting to listen anymore, I focused on trying to free my wrists even though it was draining my energy. I kept my eyes on the window, waiting to see if any other car would pass by, and I could scream for their attention. But we were going into isolated territory. There was no one around for miles. Regret started to seep in for firing all my bodyguards. I could have just kept even Adrian, at least.

Fuck my life.

Even if someone reported me missing, they wouldn't know where I'd gone. It was going to be impossible for them to find me. Fear spiked through me when the car finally stopped. There were two giant glass buildings that towered any other building I've ever seen in Howl's Edge. I wondered how the hell everyone had missed this. It should be obvious, especially if the lost omegas resided here, unless authorities were turning a blind eye to them.

Some alphas were shifted into werewolf forms, prowling around the building. Alphas were roaming everywhere. I could tell from their physique that they were alphas with heavier and huskier features.

"Welcome to your new permanent home," smiled Jordan, and my stomach twisted. "This is where you'll be producing babies for years to come."

He opened the car door, pulling me along with him.

The sand was hot under my bare feet as he walked me to the smaller building. I stared at the sand sifting through my toes as we walked. The sun was beating down mercilessly today on the island, and I couldn't bear to look at what could be my future home. I didn't even bother fighting against Jordan as he pulled me towards it with my hands tied behind my back. This place had the tightest security I'd ever seen.

"So there are only alphas here?" I commented.

"The very best," said Jordan, puffing his chest.

"So you're like the recruiter or something," I said sarcastically, hoping to infuriate him. His smug smile disappeared, and he turned to me. He lifted his hand and slapped me across the face.

It all happened in the blink of an eye.

I stood there in shock. I couldn't believe he did that. I'd never seen this side of him in the months we'd been together.

"You will respect me while you're here," he snarled. "Let's go."

My face stung from the ringing slap as he pulled me by the arm to the building.

This wasn't a joke.

He was seriously going to breed me after stalking me for days. My throat tightened with every step, and I even forgot the pain in my burning feet from the shock.

When we entered the building, I first noticed the air conditioner hitting my burning face and the cold marble floors I stood on. Three alphas stood at the door, wearing all-black uniforms with emblems of a yellow wolf-head stamped onto their shoulders. One of them carried a clipboard as two of the alphas patted me down. All I had on were my silk shorts and my tank top.

I felt uncomfortable when one of them cupped and squeezed my breast, and I tried pulling away. He had short black hair and icy gray eyes.

"We have to make sure you didn't sneak in any pills with you," he said. "We want you to be as comfortable as possible here, love."

"I'm not comfortable at all," I said. "And I never will be comfortable here."

Then he turned to Jordan, "I can take it from here."

Jordan nodded roughly as the guard untied the cloth holding my wrists together. He didn't look happy being dismissed after doing all the work of stalking me. I felt a sense of relief once Jordan was gone.

"Please keep him away from me," I said in a low voice as I watched him walk towards the other alphas on this floor.

"We try to keep him away from the omegas, but he really likes you and insists on having you. But no worries, we can try securing a different alpha handler for you," he said. "If there's not one available, you'll have him for tonight."

What? An alpha handler? I suddenly felt like a pet. It was a strange and unwelcome feeling.

"Please let me go," I said. He looked surprised at my question. Did he not have omegas ask him to leave this place before? I was mind-boggled.

"This is the best place for an omega," he said. "And the safest."

"Listen, I was kidnapped and don't belong here," I said. "You guys will be in huge trouble kidnapping omegas."

I turned my head back to look at the door, but I could see the werewolves stalking the entrance, waiting for me to escape and make a move. They'd probably tackle me in no time and rip my head off if I tried.

"Let me show you around, love," he said. "By the way, my name's Henry."

I didn't shake the hand he offered. He acted like this was normal, and my whole life upended like it didn't matter.

"Listen, I need to get back to work and back to my life," I insisted when he took my hand.

"It's okay, most omegas panic at first," he said in a calm, tranquil voice. "But once you see how stress-free it is here, you'll never want to return, my love."

"Can you stop calling me that?" I muttered.

He ignored that as he walked me up a spiraling set of stairs that led into a huge main room covered in glass. There were giant cushions everywhere with omegas lying on them. They were either lounging or talking with each other. I only got a glimpse before he led me down a hallway with many doors in either direction. Everything was white, blinding, and shiny.

"That was the Social Room you just saw," explained Henry. "You will love it here, Lacy."

I highly doubted that.

My heart was still beating fast at how dystopian everything seemed. I was sure my feet were dirty as hell as I walked on the cold, clinical floors.

"Jordan mentioned something about breeding?" I said.

"He's correct," said Henry, and my heart pounded faster as he opened the door to a room that had a red tag on the door, which he promptly removed. "This will be your room. Room fifty-six."

He handed me the red tag with the room number, and all I wanted to do was shred it to pieces. But I had to figure out what was happening. I entered the room and saw a large bed in the corner with a circular brown rug in front of it. There was an entire closet filled with clothes, a large mirror, and a dresser. The bed looked so comfortable, and I felt like I was ready to pass out on it. I yawned as I looked at it. The long road trip had worn me out to no end.

"Is there any way I can buy my freedom? I will pay you whatever you want," I offered. I couldn't have my life taken away from me just like that, and I was willing to pay any price.

"The only thing we want is to grow our island stronger with more alpha babies," he said, smiling. "Please get yourself comfortable. Then I'd like you to come to the Social Room for the presentation."

I said nothing as I watched him leave the room, quietly closing the door behind him. I walked around the room briefly, inspecting every drawer in the dresser. I saw that there were brand new intimate wear with tags on them. *Thank goodness.* The closet was filled with dresses, and lingerie. I walked into the bathroom and looked into the oval mirror above the sink. My hair was straggly and unkempt. The right side of my face displayed an angry red mark from Jordan's abuse. I touched my face, wondering what had become of me.

As I showered, I thought about all my family's emotions once they learned I had disappeared. My mother's panic would be unimaginable. She had told me she went crazy when she lost Gabe for a while when the Royal Pack took him. Maybe I could ask Henry if I could somehow send a message to my family. But talking to Henry was like talking to a robot. He ignored anything that required real answers and instead spoke of the greatness of this stupid camp.

I hopped out of the warm shower and dried myself off as I walked into the room. I needed something to wear and saw slippers of various colors on the shoe shelf. I slipped my finally clean feet into a pair of glittering black slippers. I picked out a pink dress from the closet that looked like it was my size. It had ruffled short sleeves and a gaping neckline, which revealed my cleavage. The dress was long but flowing, so it had plenty of airflow.

While combing my hair, I heard shouting outside my door.

I dropped the comb and quickly ran to the door, pressing my ear against it to hear.

Twenty-Four

LACY

I couldn't hear much of what was happening, but it sounded like a female shouting.

"No, I'm not coming out there!" she shouted.

My eyes widened when I recognized her voice. *Was Olivia here, too? What the hell was she doing here?* I softly opened my door a crack and saw that she was right across from me in room sixty-three. She looked tired, her eyes baggy, and her long black hair wild around her face.

"Leave me alone," said Olivia. "I'll come out when I'm ready."

"You need to eat," said one of the alphas. There were two of them lingering at her doorstep, holding the door open with his foot. "I'll come back to check on you."

The two alphas shook their heads as they left.

I ran to her door once I was sure the coast was clear. I knocked on her door three times as lightly as I could.

I could barely breathe from my panic. I had no idea if this was allowed or what would happen to me if they caught me here.

"Leave me alone!" she screamed.

"Olivia, it's me," I muttered. The door slammed open, and she stared at me with wide doe eyes.

"Lacy!" she screamed, vaulting herself at me. We hugged and

pulled away from each other, teary-eyed and unable to believe we found each other in this godforsaken place. "Come in, hurry."

Olivia closed the door behind us as I headed to the chair in her room and sat down. She sat on the edge of the bed, looking a little bit worse for wear and still wearing pajamas.

"How long were you in here for? How did they take you?" I asked her. I wanted to ask her a million more questions, but I had no idea how long I'd be here before we were caught.

"Right after the haunted house thing. Before I could even get into my car, three men grabbed me and put a bag over my head. I passed out and woke up here," she said, her voice breaking. "My mom's going to be beside herself."

"I know, mine too," I said. "They breed omegas in here or something."

"Every night, alphas will come into your room to *cuddle you*," said Olivia, and my stomach dropped. "It's to bring you to heat. I had my first night yesterday. I wore myself out trying to wrestle them off me, and I ended up sleeping between them."

"Oh god," I said, feeling sick. *Was Jordan going to be in my room tonight?* If so, I had no idea how I would escape him. He was adamant about being my 'handler' apparently.

"Why were you screaming at the alphas just now?"

"They were the ones who cuddled me all night, and they came back to check on me," said Olivia. "They want to make sure we're healthy and happy, mingling with everyone."

"What the hell?"

"It's sick, isn't it?"

"We need to find a way out of this fucking place," I said. "I think we should go to the social room and talk to the other omegas. Figure this place out so we can find a way out of here."

Olivia sighed, running her hand over her messy brown hair. "Yeah, you're right. Let me get dressed. Don't go anywhere, okay?"

"I won't," I promised as I grabbed the comb from her

assigned dresser. "I'll be right here until you're done, and then we can go together."

⁓

THE SOCIAL ROOM, as they called it, was a beautiful sunlit room surrounded by glass windows. There were huge vases of flowers in every corner, creating such a feminine atmosphere as I walked around with Olivia. I longed to lay on the massage tables and get pampered, but I had to see what was going on. Most of the omegas stared at us as we walked in to meet our kind.

I had never seen so many omegas gathered in one place before. I only knew a few omegas in my close-knit group of friends.

To see fifty of them in one room was astonishing to me. Different omega scents flooded the air, all flowery and light. My scent was the most boring, and I hoped no one would notice among all the other scents.

"God, it's overpowering in here," said Olivia, wrinkling her nose. "There aren't any scent blockers for anyone to put on either."

"I know," I said. "Damn, look at the food table."

There were two tables lined with sweets that omegas typically enjoyed. The different flavored ice creams immediately caught my eye, and my mouth watered. I was for sure going to grab that later. But I was hungry for something real after the long car ride, so I poured the hot, steamy food onto my plate. While picking out the food, a feeling of sadness and homesickness washed over me.

I missed Ryder, and I was shocked at myself for feeling that.

"Girl, are you just grabbing everything?" said Olivia.

"I don't care," I said. "They're the ones who kidnapped us. They might as well feed us good."

"Haha," said Olivia, stacking her plate with a massive scoop of rice.

After we sufficiently piled our plates with food, we found an empty cushion in this giant social room. As we sat and ate, I was mostly on alert that we'd get dragged away anytime to get knotted and bred. But as I observed the omegas, they all looked...relaxed. Relaxed, pampered, and fed. I didn't like any of this one bit.

"I was so hungry," said Olivia. "But I refused to eat anything when I first arrived here."

"You mean, you didn't eat anything from the time you got here?" I asked, shocked. I barely survived today, especially after the long, hot car ride.

"Nope," said Olivia. "I was on edge until you knocked on my door. Now I'm more relaxed and not so alone, you know?"

Tears pricked my eyes. Olivia wasn't one to get all mushy like this, and for her to open up like this was a big deal.

"You're going to make me cry," I said, smiling through my tears. "We'll get out of here, one way or another."

"I know," she said, her eyes glistening. "I'll be counting the days until that happens."

I began to wonder if there was any hope at all, but I had to say it for her comfort, at least. Realistically, I didn't think anyone would look for me unless my family tried to visit me or heard about me on the news. Ben and Ty would probably contact my family if I didn't show up to work. That was that, at least.

"Good evening, omegas," announced Henry, walking into the Social Room. A few omegas giggled, and a few waved at him. They all looked delighted to meet him, and I wondered if he knotted any of them. The thought suddenly grossed me out.

"Ugh, it's like a cult," I said.

"Tell me about it," said Olivia.

"I want to welcome our newest arrivals," said Henry, his eyes on me. "Our job as alphas is to ensure you are all comfortable and well-taken care of. We aim to produce the healthiest alpha babies on Howl's Edge."

I looked over at Olivia, who was rolling her eyes.

"He didn't need to kidnap us for that."

"But not only that," continued Henry in a louder voice. I was sure he could hear Olivia with his powerful alpha hearing. "Many of you have found a better home here than anywhere else in the real world. In here, you could live out your full omega potential. Nesting, breeding, and being shown all the love and cuddles in the world."

I could hear all the sighs of contentment from the omegas in the room. It was a dream life of many omegas, but not *my* dream. I wanted to sing. I didn't want to end up giving birth to a bunch of babies and never see my family again.

I didn't realize my hand was raised until Henry called on me.

"What if we're not interested in having babies? How can we go back home to our families?" I said boldly and loudly. This time, he had to answer me. There was no evading the question. Not in front of fifty omegas. Some omegas looked shocked that I would ask that question and be so disrespectful to an alpha.

"If you are not happy here, we can chat later about how we can improve," said Henry, oblivious to my rising frustration. He somehow avoided answering me altogether. "I'm going to go over a few rules here. At nine p.m., everyone should be in their rooms, awaiting their alpha handlers. They will spend the night with you to try and bring you to heat. Please let me know if you are in heat. The alpha handlers will immediately care for you before you go into further pain from your heat."

Take care? As in knotting, I thought snidely.

He left after his speech, and the room was once again filled with chatter. I wondered how all these omegas were freaking happy. This wasn't good at all.

"I want to talk to these omegas," said Olivia after we finished our plates and washed our hands in the bathroom down the hall. When we returned, she eyed two blond omegas who looked like they were related. "Hi, may we sit with you?"

"Sure," said one of them with gentle grace as she patted the blue circle cushion. It was roomy, and there was space for five to sit. The second omega didn't look thrilled to see us there, and she looked wary. They looked similar to each other and in their twenties.

CRAVED BY THE PACK

"How long have you ladies been here?" asked Olivia. "We're new."

"A year," said the one who invited us to sit. "I'm Julie."

"My name's Olivia. Are you two related?"

"Yes, I'm her younger sister," said the second omega. "My name's Treasure." They both looked at me expectantly.

"I'm Lacy," I said, and their eyes widened.

"*The* Lacy from Electric Rose?" asked Julie. "I knew you looked familiar."

"I look a little rough without makeup," I shrugged.

"You're beautiful," said Treasure.

"Thank you, you too," I said, smiling. We needed them to open up to us about this terrible camp. "So, are you both happy living here?"

"Yes," said Julie. "Our lives were a mess before we were taken. Our mother hated that she had omega girls. She kept us hidden away our entire lives and screamed at us constantly. I'm glad we're here, especially for my little sister."

"Were you kidnapped?" asked Olivia.

"Julie heard about the camp from someone, and we pretty much signed up," said Treasure. "At least we don't starve here."

"How about the breeding thing? What do you think about that?" asked Olivia. Just then, we were interrupted by Henry.

"May I speak with you for a moment, Lacy?" he requested.

"Sure," I said, not having a choice. We were essentially stuck here with a bunch of brainwashed omegas with no chance of escape. I followed him to the side of the room.

"What can we do to make you more comfortable?" he asked.

"To let me go so I can live my life," I said. "I don't want to have babies."

"Unfortunately, that's not possible," he sighed. "I also wanted to tell you how much we appreciate having you here. You're an inspiration to many omegas here who know you. Many of them feel a lot more comfortable now that they've seen even the most popular omega here."

"I don't give a fuck about that. I'll pay any price to leave."

He blinked at my vehement words.

"You'll soon see that our goal here is what you need," said Henry, coming closer to me. His alpha scent washed over me with his nearness, and I refused to fall victim to it. "Just let your true omega instincts take over."

He touched my cheek with the tip of his finger, and I swallowed nervously. I could already feel the slick dripping down my thighs at the contact.

Twenty-Five

LACY

My stomach was in knots as I lay in bed on my first night here. I didn't want to be here at all, but I didn't have a choice as I waited for my assigned alphas to enter my room.

All day, Olivia and I enjoyed the spa. I had pedicures and even had my hair done by the many hair stylists here. There were so many secret rooms with different services that I thought I was on vacation. I forgot why I was here until 9 o'clock hit, and everything was shut down.

We were reluctant to go into our rooms until some of the guards demanded we go into our room for the night. That was the first time I saw them getting annoyed at us. So I was wearing pajamas now with the most coverage even though it still showed all my thighs and arms. I couldn't close my eyes and sleep as I waited for the impending doom.

I heard the bedroom door open, and my heart pounded faster. I stared at the forms of two hulking males in the dark, and when they came nearer, I could make out the face of Jordan and another alpha I had never seen before. They wore just black robes with nothing on underneath. I shivered in disgust, seeing their bare chests.

I wanted to puke.

"Hello, Pinkie," said Jordan. His voice was the most evil voice I've ever heard. I could swear it never sounded like that before.

"Can't I get assigned a different alpha, please?" I said.

"Are you still refusing me even now?" asked Jordan, eyebrows raised as he approached the bed. He stopped at the edge of it.

"Why would you think I'd want you?"

"Come here," said Jordan, pulling me by the hand out of bed. He wasn't waiting one bit. "Remove all your clothes. As you know, this is when we bring you to heat. If not tonight, it'll be through several sessions, which I'm sure you'll enjoy."

I stood in the middle of the room, surrounded by these males who were staring at me like I was their last meal. *Why didn't they bother some other omega who wanted this?*

"Jordan, please, I know you're not like this," I said. "You would never hurt me."

He tilted his head to one side, smirking, and I knew I had lost him completely, and the Jordan that I knew from before was completely erased.

"I'm not going to say it again, Lacy," he said.

With shaking fingers, I removed my tank top, and I could feel their gazes burn onto my skin as they stared at my breasts. I couldn't look up at them as I gripped the waistband of my shorts and panties, letting them slide to the floor. I stepped out of it and placed a hand over my pussy to cover myself. With my other arm, I covered my chest as much as possible.

But I knew it was in vain.

"We're going to touch you. This step is for you to get used to us," said the second alpha.

He had short green hair and a piercing in one ear. He was short but stocky. My chest was heaving with panic as he ran a callused thumb down my left arm. Jordan was to my right, and he rubbed my thighs. His hand trailed across both thighs, gripping and releasing. Their alpha scent wasn't desirable to me. All I smelt was cigarettes from them and liquor. I despised every second of this, and now I knew why I never wanted to give up my virginity to Jordan while I quickly gave it away to Ryder.

Oh, Ryder...the thought of him made me want to cry. *He just wanted to protect me from this.*

"Your cheeks are pink, and you're breathing so hard," said Jordan soothingly. But his voice was anything but soothing to me. "Let's get you over to the bed, sweetheart."

They each held me by the hand and walked me to the bed. Every step felt like death to me.

"Are you going to knot me or something?" I asked, hating how shaky my voice sounded to my ears.

"Not until you go into heat," said Jordan, watching me as I lay on the bed on my side. He untied the rope around his bathrobe and lay in front of me while his comrade snuggled up behind me. I could feel his thick, hairy thighs brushing against the back of my legs.

I was mildly relieved they weren't going to knot me tonight. Especially since I hadn't had my heat suppressant pills for hours now. I was pretty sure it was wearing off, and if I was to get knotted, it was immediate pregnancy. An alpha's knot ensured an omega got pregnant, with not one drop of semen going to waste due to the knotting. But the most fertile time for an omega was during their heat. I was deathly afraid of that happening.

"How long does it take an omega to go into heat without her pills?" I asked as his hands roamed over my side, eventually rubbing my breasts.

My pulse rate increased with every touch, no matter how hard I tried to fight it- I was getting horny from the touching and cuddling. The alpha behind me was rubbing my butt and squeezing my thighs. Every touch felt foreign to me and unwelcome.

This was unlike the feelings I had with my bodyguards. *Former bodyguards.*

I was horny, but I also felt sick to my stomach.

"Typically two to five days with help from the alphas," said

Jordan, circling my belly with his finger. "Are you getting excited at the thought? Omegas love getting knotted during their heats. You're going to be so wild for my cock."

"No, I'm not," I said, breathing harder. I wanted to be anywhere else but here. His finger dipped lower, tracing the triangle patch between my legs. My omega body betrayed me when he stuck his finger between my legs. He smiled when he felt the slick coating my pussy lips.

"Are you sure you're not excited?" he asked. The alpha behind me started breathing into my neck, purring to keep me calm while his hand gripped my ass cheeks like nothing else mattered.

"Please stop, Jordan," I begged. "I don't want to do this."

"You're made to serve alphas," he crooned into my ear as his finger wiggled upwards inside me. More wetness seeped between my legs, betraying the control I tried to maintain. "In today's society, omegas think they have all these rights. But in reality, you're made to go into heat. To get fucked and knotted repeatedly to bear babies for us."

"That's not true," I gasped when his finger hit my g spot.

"Oh, you know it's true," he said. "Listen to your true omega self. You can see how true it is by the way your body craves it. Just relax and let us breed you. Your stressful career is over now. Just relax, baby."

"Please," I moaned when he plunged a second finger inside.

"Hmm...please what?" he asked, lazily circling my clit with his thumb while his other finger was inside me. "I never put my foot down enough. And now you're begging me to be inside you. Isn't that right, darling?"

"No!" I shouted, trying to pull away. I could not let him make me orgasm. If I allowed it, it meant I was giving in. But the second alpha gripped my thigh and lifted it, opening me further for Jordan's ministrations. I tried to pull away, but his grip made escape impossible. My chest was rising and falling from arousal, and my pussy was clenching, waiting for the release he'd give me.

But I couldn't give in.

"Hold her leg open," commanded Jordan as he continued to rub my clit with his thumb. I tried to pull his hand off my thigh, but it was impossible to pry his fingers off. Jordan pinned me onto the bed with his mouth on my neck, and if I moved, I'd suffocate. His hot, shallow breathing covered my skin as he thrust his fingers in and out of me. "You're not a virgin anymore, and I should've been the one to take your virginity. But at least I will be the one to put a baby in you."

"No, you won't," I said, gasping as my stomach clenched and an orgasm rocked through my body. Tears of disappointment ran down my face as my body shook and trembled with mini after-shocks from my orgasm. I felt like dying in this moment. This was so humiliating on a whole other level.

After the pleasure came shame.

They released me, and Jordan removed his fingers from me, licking his fingers slowly.

"She came," said the alpha behind me.

"I've always wanted to taste you," Jordan said. Anger and shock rolled through me as I lay shaking on my back while the alphas stroked my body. I closed my eyes, wishing for this nightmare to end. "We'll allow you to rest for a bit, then we'll do it again, Pinkie. You did such a good job, just don't fight Brett and I. It'll be even more fun that way."

Fuck my life.

"I need to use the bathroom," I said, getting off the bed. Upon closing the door behind me, which didn't have a lock- I collapsed on the floor, holding my face between my hands as I cried. I cried for giving in to Jordan's touch. Tears drenched my hands as I sat there broken. He completely ruined my life, and I had never felt so dejected as I did now. It was miserable, and I felt sick to my stomach.

I needed to escape. I started to feel sad for Olivia and all the other omegas who didn't want to be here.

"Pinkie?" asked Jordan when he opened the door, seeing me crying on the floor.

I removed my hands from my face and looked up at him through my tears.

"You're a monster. A horrible monster," I shouted.

He swallowed as he took in the sight of my miserable self sitting on the floor of this cold bathroom.

"Most omegas need time to adjust," he said without emotion. "Perfectly normal."

"I will always hate you," I said. "No matter what happens. Even if I have your baby, I will despise you until the day I die."

He looked taken aback, blinking twice. "I'll give you some time to process, and then we'll continue. You will beg for my knot before your heat even begins. I'd like to see you back in bed in five minutes - no excuses."

He slammed the door shut, and I shuddered. I've made him angry, but I didn't care. I didn't have anything to lose now. Getting up from the floor on weak, shaking legs, I washed my face and dried myself with the towel. I stared into the mirror. My eyes had dark bags under them, and my hair was messy. A far cry from when I was confident and happy in my life, ready to sing for whoever would listen.

I remembered my mother and her struggles when she had Gabe taken away from her. She had been sold at an auction after they took her baby, going through much worse than I did. And I could hear her voice clear as day in my head to get through this until I could escape.

Be strong, Lacy.

So I gritted my teeth and walked back into the dark bedroom.

Twenty-Six
‿◠◡◠‿

RYDER

"I really think we should check on Lacy," said Adrian as he paced around the field. My pack had become despondent, and I started feeling gloomy since we left Lacy. We'd get over her after a few days, but that wasn't the case. I wiped the sweat from my forehead with a handkerchief.

Every day, I felt the emptiness of her presence. At night, when I imagined another male approaching her- I'd feel sick to my stomach. But she didn't want me, not after my punishment of her.

"Your stubbornness and her anger issues clash. Like two magnets repelling each other," said Cooper as he put on his earmuffs before shooting the target at the end of the field.

"But he can *simply* apologize," said Ethan gruffly. "Now we're waiting around for another guard duty job, wasting our time when we could be hunting the stalker."

"She's not our problem anymore," I said, trying to end this unending conversation we always seem to fall into during training. The day we left Lacy's house, my boss scolded me for my stubbornness and the harsh discipline of a fun-loving omega.

Yes, maybe I shouldn't have put my hands on her.

"Does it hurt to check on her, though?" said Adrian, not

153

letting this go, and I sighed. Some part of my soul wanted to get a glimpse of her again, even though she screamed at me furiously.

"It doesn't hurt," I said, rubbing my hand over my head.

"Fuck yes," said Lucas, smiling. To get a reaction out of Lucas was a big thing, and we all smiled as we looked over at him lifting weights on a bench.

"I'm guessing we're all in agreement then?"

"Let's fucking go already," said Ethan, and every man dropped what they were holding.

I shook my head as we headed to our armored truck. I grinned as I followed behind them. I wanted to apologize and do everything else necessary to see her beautiful face again. Or at least end as friends. This non-communication was hurting me and my pack. *But was I ready for her ultimate rejection of me?* I knew I didn't look like the typical alpha she'd date, but I had to try at least.

∼

WHEN WE PULLED up to Lacy's house- confusion set in when we saw the open gate.

"She wouldn't leave the gate open just like that," said Lucas. We all sat up in alarm, and I immediately dialed her number on my phone. I tried calling her once on our way to her house, but she didn't answer. I assumed she was still angry at me.

I hopped out when Adrian parked the truck, as adrenaline flowed through my body. I jogged to her front door and knocked.

No answer.

I rang the doorbell, standing there for a few seconds. Nothing.

"Call her band or something if anyone has the number," I told my pack. If she had simply forgotten to close the gate, it wouldn't be a problem. But in my gut, I knew something was off. I looked around the door for anything that could be off, but as I twisted the doorknob, I realized it was open.

Shit.

She would never leave the door unlocked. Guns out, we carefully walked inside.

"We need to split up and see if she's anywhere. Try not to be loud in case he's here holding her in one of the rooms," I said. We all split in different directions, and I immediately bounded up the stairs to her room. The door was wide open, and my heart sank when I saw her messy bed and broken lamp. She would never leave her things in disarray like this.

Something terrible happened when I left her. Every second I spent here meant she was suffering somewhere else. I saw her phone on the bed and carefully walked inside, not wanting to destroy any evidence. Picking up the phone, I saw a bunch of missed calls over the last several days.

After watching her put in the password several times, I logged into it and quickly went through her call log. Her mother, who looked exactly like her, had called the most, and someone named Aunt Jade had called her also.

I called her cousin Olivia first since she knew about us working for Lacy. No answer. Now I was really getting worried about this omega. Next, I called Jade before calling Lacy's mother. I had to gather as much information as possible before reaching out to her.

"Hello," said Jade. Her voice was frantic and sounded like she'd been crying.

"Hello, Jade?" I said.

"Who's this?" she asked, sounding panicked. "Are you the kidnapper? I can't reach my daughter Olivia or Lacy. What did you do to our girls?!"

"I'm not the kidnapper," I said amidst her yelling. It took her a minute before she decided to start listening. "I'm Lacy's bodyguard, and I can't find her anywhere. Do you have a clue of where she might be?"

"Well, you did a poor fucking job guarding her," said Jade and I sighed. "Her mother is worried sick as well and at my house. She said she'd been at Lacy's house and..."

"Let me talk to him," said another female voice. Good, this was probably Lacy's mother. She did *not* sound happy. "Hello, guard, I'm Vanessa. Lacy's mother."

"I'm Ryder," I said. "I don't have much time. I need to find her."

"Please tell me what happened," said Vanessa, sounding like she was on the verge of tears. "I can't lose another baby of mine. I couldn't sleep for days. Why haven't you been able to guard her?"

"She fired us," I sighed. "Listen, we're doing everything we can."

"I always told her that her temper will be her downfall," said Vanessa, sighing. "Olivia is also missing. We tried calling both of them. Our husbands are out searching the entire island as well."

"I will do my best," I reassured both mothers before hanging up. I could feel the pain in their voices and the urgency.

We had to find Lacy first and foremost.

"Damn," said Cooper, who was listening to everything at the door.

I rubbed my face with frustration.

"Where the fuck did he take her?!" I shouted as I paced around the room. I was tempted to rush out and knock down every door on the island to find her. But if we ran around willy-nilly around the island, it would waste more time. She was probably scared to death. I remembered how she hugged me when we came to her rescue once. And the relief in her eyes upon seeing me.

Looking at her phone, I called Olivia's number again. It was useless trying that.

"If Lacy and Olivia were taken to the same location, that would be crazy," said Cooper.

"Wait...if they're in the same location," I said, my mind spinning. "Think you can trace Olivia's phone?"

~

I COULDN'T BELIEVE it when we found the location tracing the phone. The drive took two hours, leading us to a remote location.

The two glass buildings looked like it was in the middle of the fucking desert with no hint of civilization around. It was guarded by a formidable perimeter of coiled barbed wire and vigilant security detail in every corner. We stopped the truck on the side of the road.

"I'll take just Ethan with me," I told them.

"What the hell?" said Cooper.

I've heard of operations like this. These were different types of alphas. They were elitists who looked down on every other type of werewolf. I didn't want to take the risk, but I didn't want to tell him that either.

"It'll draw less attention, and I'd like the oldest to accompany me," I said, staring at the barrier and werewolves prowling. They hadn't seen us since we parked farther away, but they'd see us immediately once we started walking. "I'll give you a call once we get Lacy and Olivia out of there. We only came for Lacy, but I promised Olivia's mom."

"Don't do anything reckless," said Adrian. "I swear if you mess anything up..."

"I won't," I said. "Wait for my call or text."

"Do you even have a plan, or are you just going to barge in there?" asked Lucas.

No. I didn't have a plan, but my pack didn't need to know that.

"Just standby. If we get trapped for longer than three days, send in reinforcements. Tell our boss what happened."

"Three days?!" said Adrian. "We need to buy more snacks and food."

"Alright, see you, Ryder," said Lucas, clapping me on the back. "Be careful out there."

Ethan and I walked around the armored van and along the walkway to the camp. There was only one entrance between the barbed wire. A tall gate guarded by four werewolves fully shifted into werewolf forms, and two alpha guards had their guns out upon seeing us.

"What's your business here?" called one of them, aiming directly at me.

My pulse pounded as I raised my arms above my head. I had left all my weapons back in the van just in case. I didn't want to seem like a threat. I was here to pick up my Lacy and go home.

That was all there was to it.

I stopped walking, and so did Ethan, who also had his hands up.

"We're wondering if you had any room for us to join," I said. The two guards looked at each other, debating whether or not to let us in. I had no idea what this place was, only that it was surrounded by fucking alphas, and they had some evil purpose for taking omegas.

"Did Henry call for you?" asked one of the guards.

"He did," said Ethan in a loud voice, trying to sound as confident as possible.

"Oh, alright," said one of them, allowing us to walk through the compound.

Shit, I couldn't believe that fucking worked. But this operation was dangerous as fuck, and anything could go wrong at any time.

The sand flew in my face as we walked closer to the main building covered in glass. When we walked towards the building, we were stopped by another guard at the door.

"We're here to see Henry," I said immediately, and the guard spoke into a device he was holding.

A few minutes passed, and we were ushered inside to an office. The person sitting behind the desk was tall and with short black hair. I immediately sensed the evil emanating from this dude, who had a kind smile plastered on his face.

A smile of pure evil.

"I know I didn't invite you here," Henry said. "But please... sit."

Twenty-Seven

RYDER

We sat in the two chairs in front of his desk while he watched us closely with crossed hands.

"So, what is your real purpose being here?" said Henry.

I licked my lips, hoping to seem as genuine as possible. If I said our real purpose, he may never let Lacy leave. I had to be as discreet as possible with this alpha. He could set his guards on us any time, killing us in the middle of nowhere.

"I was hoping I could join you," I said, trying not to state what for. Because I had no fucking clue what they did here.

"I don't think that's true," said Henry. "Is your true goal to impregnate omegas or to infiltrate? Did the government send you?"

"I don't fucking agree with anything the government does," I said, horrified to think that Lacy could be walking around pregnant right now.

"Hmm, how do I believe that?" he said. "We have caught an alpha or two here trying to sneak out omegas. What makes you think I'll trust you?"

"There's no way to know that," I said. "It's fine if you don't

159

want two extra alphas to join your team here. I want to help, and it's my life's mission. If you do not wish to accept us, that's okay."

His face looked deep in thought at that statement. He looked like he was starting to believe me.

Good.

"Alright, let me tell you a little about this place, and you can determine if it interests you."

～

LATER THAT DAY, Henry gave us matching uniforms that every alpha was wearing at this place. I was shocked to hear that this was an actual camp to breed omegas, and I never heard of such a thing until now. But of course, we nodded and agreed with everything he said like it wasn't the most outrageous, sickening thing I've heard in my life.

Everywhere he walked us, my eyes scanned every room for Lacy's long red hair down her back. But I didn't see her anywhere.

"Now, this is the Heat Observation Room," said Henry, leading us into a room also covered in glass. The room was filled with computers and chairs that alphas were sitting in. It was a sizeable room, and on the other side, I could see females lounging unknowingly on cushions and getting pampered. My gaze naturally roamed for Lacy. "On the other side of this glass, you can see all the omegas in the Social Room. We can see them, but they can't see us."

"Why is that?" asked Ethan, and I nudged him on the elbow. We needed the least attention to us as possible. There were alphas staring daggers at us, hoping we wouldn't take their assigned omegas.

"Our job is to observe the omegas for signs of their heat. Fainting, fatigue, flushed faces, or signs of pain," said Henry. "A lot of them will try to hide it, but they've been trained to look for the signs."

"And if they're in heat?" I asked.

"We assign a group of alphas to knot her as soon as possible. It's the prime time to create alpha babies," said Henry with an excited gleam in his eyes.

"Interesting," I said as we walked around the room. "Then what happens after they give birth? Do you let them leave?"

"Of course not," said Henry, shaking his head vehemently. "We take the babies to foster care in the city, and then the cycle starts again."

"So we just need to breed them," I said. This was a sick operation. I was thinking about how archaic this whole thing was. Poor Lacy must be going mad right now. I had to figure out a way to get to her, no matter what.

"The pure-bred alpha wolves are stronger," said Henry with a maniacal grin. "The island needs us, Ryder. And with your help, we'll become the greatest nation on this planet."

Twenty-Eight

LACY

The next morning, I was relieved to wake up to an empty bed. I yawned, remembering the horror from the last night. Jordan took pleasure in making me orgasm at his fingertips repeatedly until I collapsed from exhaustion. According to Henry's rules, the alphas weren't allowed to do that unless the omega wasn't going into heat fast enough. It was supposed to be strictly cuddling for the pheromones.

Frustration boiled within me as I showered and put on clothes for the day. I planned to complain to Henry and force him to change my alpha handlers. I hated Jordan more and more with a passion. Deciding to go with a plain beige dress, I threw it on, hoping to look as dull and unappealing as possible. It flared at my waist, stopping at my thighs. I tied my hair up in a ponytail and in the mirror, realizing how drab I looked.

My eyes were baggy from all my sobbing last night, and my face was puffy. I put on a little bit of lip gloss and some eyeliner so I could look halfway decent when I hung out in the Social Room today. But first, I had to see Olivia and make sure she was okay.

I wore plain white slippers and carefully opened my door, checking to see if there was anyone before I left my room.

Walking across the hallway, a flood of emotion overcame me. I

162

stood in front of her door, imagining the horrors that she was going through, too. Tears fell down my face as I sobbed in the hallway. Memories of how gruff Jordan was without a shred of care and how he slapped me reminded me of the monster he was.

I had to collect myself, so I took a few deep breaths, resting against the wall.

I sniffled, and I suddenly felt a hand wrap over my mouth.

Panic shot through me. My breathing quickened, but the scent of the alpha holding me was different. A familiar, calming smell that I knew all too well.

"Don't scream or talk loud," said Ryder in a harsh whisper. "I'm going to let you go now."

He released my mouth, and I spun around to see Ryder. Relief and joy flowed through every vein of my being. I honestly couldn't remember a time when I was more relieved to see someone more than today. Despite my hesitations about him, I wanted to hug and kiss him so badly. But I couldn't give away his cover.

He was wearing an all-black uniform, just like all the alpha guards here. A shirt, black pants, a silver belt, and the wolf badge on his shoulder.

"How did you find me?" I whispered, looking down the hallway to make sure no one was coming.

"Don't worry about that," he said quickly, looking back and forth. "I just want to let you know that I'm here for you. Sit tight, and don't cry, okay? We'll bust you out of here very soon, Lacy."

"I'm sorry for everything," I said as remorse flowed through me. I didn't want him to leave, and I felt panic at the thought.

"It's okay, sweetheart, I'm sorry too," he said, his eyes on my lips. "Why were you crying? What did they fucking do to you?"

"I.."

My heart palpitated as he neared me. I wanted him to kiss me so badly. More in this moment than any other. But we were soon interrupted by alpha guards, and I had to pretend not to know him as I quickly turned away from him.

He left down the hall, joining the other alphas. He turned back one last time to look at me, and my heart palpitated at the promising look in his eyes. I quickly scurried into Olivia's room. Olivia looked at me wide-eyed as she was combing her hair.

"Hey, girl," said Olivia, watching me through the mirror as I shut the door.

"Oh my god, we might be able to leave this place," I babbled.

"Slow down a minute," said Olivia, dropping her comb on the ground. "Tell me everything."

"Ryder's here," I said excitedly. I felt much lighter and happier than I had in hours. I didn't realize how the presence of a certain alpha could lift my spirits so much. "I don't know when we're leaving, but at least he knows we're here."

"Thank god," sighed Olivia. Even she looked like the weight of the world just dropped from her shoulders. "We're so fucking lucky."

"I know," I said. "Let's go eat. Suddenly, I'm like real hungry."

"Me too."

~

AFTER EATING breakfast in the Social Room with Olivia and her new friends, I decided to go downstairs and see if there was a chance I could see Ryder again. It was probably irresponsible, but I knew there were always alphas roaming around downstairs.

"I'll be right back," I told Olivia as she chatted with the two sisters. She nodded to me. I could tell there was a new glow to her now that there was a chance we were going to escape. I was also excited but very impatient as I slowly walked down the staircase. Just as I guessed, there were quite a few alphas down here. I looked around for Henry to tell him about Jordan's mistreatment, but I was also secretly looking for Ryder.

"What do you need?" asked an alpha as he spied me coming down the stairs.

"I'm looking for Henry. I have a complaint," I said.

"Oh, he's right over there," he said, pointing to the general gathering of alphas who were conversing in low voices and standing around.

My stomach flipped when I saw Ethan with his long, scruffy beard. He saw me, too, from across the room and winked. I smiled instantly. I was so happy to see him there, and the familiar feeling of warmth pricked my belly. Our last intimate time together was the hottest thing I'd ever experienced.

Suddenly, I felt a hard grip on my arm.

I looked over my shoulder, panicked to see Jordan and his angry red face.

"Come with me," he said. He dragged me to one of the rooms nearby and slammed the door. My heart was beating so fast I wanted to cry with fear. I was never so scared in my life. "I saw you smiling at the new guy."

"I was just being polite," I said, my eyes on the ground. I didn't want to escalate things now. I was almost out of this stupid place and regretting ever coming down here to see Ryder. I would have all the time to see Ryder later.

Jordan's spittle flew in my face as he neared me. His grip tightened on my arm until I felt like he would break it.

"*I'm* your alpha handler. Do you get that, bitch?"

"Yes," I whispered. "I'm sorry."

~

Ethan

I WAS SURPRISED to see Lacy in the flesh when she came down those stairs. Her beautiful delicate features in her simple yet sexy beige dress made my cock hard as soon as I set eyes on her. She was here and alive.

I winked at her when she saw me, and I delighted in her joy of seeing me. I was glad she didn't hate us anymore, thank fuck. But when I looked back, I saw some other alpha dragging her off into a room.

"Excuse me," I said to the alphas, who were in the middle of introducing themselves to me. They looked affronted that I would stop them, but I didn't fucking care. I had to know if my Lacy was alright. I rushed to the room she was held in and saw him angry and shouting at her. I smelled her scent of fear at being yelled at by this abusive alpha.

"Hey! What did she do to you?" I asked, even though the sight of his hand on her arm made me want to rip him to shreds. He was causing my omega distress. He released her and turned his rage on me instead.

Good.

Because if he touched me, I was going to kill him. I didn't give a fuck. All gloves would be off. I positioned myself in the middle of them, so if he had to touch her, he'd have to go through me. And that wasn't going to happen.

"She belongs to me," he said, eyes flashing.

Anger bubbled in my throat. My hands clenched as I tried to keep calm.

"Then why are you shouting at her?"

"I can shout at her if I want," he said smugly. "Stay away from her. She's never going to be yours. This bitch belongs to me."

My fist struck his face within seconds.

The next thing I knew was that he was on the ground. I knelt over him, repeatedly punching his face as he tried to shove me off.

No one disrespected my omega.

Lacy's screams sounded distant to me. I was held in a fog of rage. Every punch to his weasely face was glorious. The warm blood trickling off my knuckles, satisfying with every crunch.

"Fuck you," I yelled with intense rage until someone pulled me off him. "Don't you ever call her that. You're the biggest bitch I've ever seen."

Twenty-Nine

LACY

That same night, I lay in my bed wondering what had become of Ethan.

I was shocked to see him get so angry on my behalf, but I was also touched. I smiled when I remembered Ethan cursing out Jordan. The alpha security had broken up the fight, and as I stood there in shock, I saw the annoyance on Ryder's face as Ethan was dragged out of the room. Jordan's nose looked broken, bleeding everywhere when they rushed him out.

After that incident, I didn't dare look at Ryder to give away his cover, and I hung out with the omegas in the Social Room for the rest of the day.

There was nothing to do but relax and be pampered all day while I anxiously waited to hear news about Ethan. But the entire day, I heard nothing. Nothing from Ryder either, and when he would break me out of here.

I was lying naked in bed, waiting to see if Jordan would come in or if he was too injured. I hoped to moons he was too hurt to come in here. I was clutching the sheets which was pulled up to my chest as I closed my eyes. It was about that time when someone was supposed to show up. Last night was a pure nightmare, and I dreaded going through it again.

The door squeaked open, and my breathing quickened.

I felt the bed sink on both sides of me as two alphas settled in. The familiar scent of leather hit my nose, and I smiled. I opened my eyes to see Ryder lying in front of me, and I felt Ethan's beard brush my shoulder as he held me from behind.

"Don't be scared," said Ryder.

"How...how did you?"

I was at a loss for words, but I was also relieved and excited to see him here after avoiding him all day. I missed him and his pack, even though I didn't admit that to him yet.

"It was tough," said Ryder. "After Ethan's blunder, I thought we blew our cover completely. But when Ethan told them that Jordan was abusing you, they gave you over to us."

"Oh, thank goodness," I said, whispering just in case the cameras on the ceiling could hear us. The little red light blinking in the dark reminded me to be careful. "I know who the stalker is."

"Jordan?" hissed Ethan.

"Yes," I said.

"I should've let Ethan kill him then," said Ryder, sighing as he lay still beside me. "I need to touch you in case anyone is watching through the cameras. Is that okay, Lacy?"

"Yes," I said without hesitation. I missed him, and I missed his touch especially. He laid a hand on my arm as we talked for several minutes, catching up. He told me about talking to my mom on the phone and being at my house. "Do you have a plan on how we're going to get out of here?"

"I do, but it's vague," said Ryder. "I've seen alpha handlers walk omegas around the compound, and I was thinking we could try that tomorrow morning. Then we make a run for it."

"Ooh," I said, feeling excited now. I was so ready to go back home. "But we need to take Olivia too."

"I'll try, but my priority is you," said Ryder, rubbing my belly over the sheets. Ethan was rubbing my back, his hot breaths on my neck. It made my skin tingle and my pussy throb. Ryder pulled the sheet down, and his eyes widened upon seeing my nude body. "Why aren't you wearing pajamas?"

I gulped as I saw his cock straining against his black bathrobe. They were both wearing a bathrobe, naked underneath, as all the alphas wore around here during their night shift.

"They require us to be naked," I said, breathing hard as he pulled the sheets down further, and he got in underneath with me.

His eyes roamed the length of my body.

Ethan tugged on my shoulder until I lay on my back between them, naked and covered with the sheets but with them under it with me. I placed a hand over my throbbing pussy, shy for them to look. I was shaved everywhere, but I was still shy around them, even though both had knotted me.

"Did they hurt you?"

"Last night," I started to say, but my voice shook. I never expected to cry, but I could already feel the waterworks approaching.

"What happened last night, sweetheart?" asked Ryder, his hand steady over my belly, warm and comforting. I could hear Ethan muttering to himself that he wished he had killed Jordan when he got the chance.

"The stalker, but he's also my ex-boyfriend Jordan," I said. "He wouldn't stop touching me even though I cried for him to stop."

I couldn't look at Ryder or Ethan. I could already feel their energy changing to hostile anger.

"He's a sick fuck," said Ryder.

"It's okay now," I said in a lighter voice. I didn't want them to be angry right now. "I'm so happy you're here now. You have no idea how relieved I feel."

"We should have come sooner. Adrian was fucking right for once," growled Ethan, rubbing my arm.

"Aww, I miss Adrian," I said, smiling and trying to lighten the mood. I couldn't let my mood damper them coming here. Ryder kissed away my tears that I didn't know rolled down my face. I was touched that Adrian still thought of me and wanted to see how I was.

"It's alphas like your ex that ruin it for the rest of us," said Ryder. "Not all of us are like that."

"I know," I said, letting out a long, shuddering breath.

For a few minutes, we were quiet as we listened to doors opening and closing down the hall. I listened to the alphas breathing beside me. It felt nice to have them beside me, and I felt much safer than I had in days. I felt bad for Olivia, who was probably suffering with some alpha jerk in her room, but she said he wasn't that bad. He simply cuddled her every night without violating her. I didn't tell her my experience with Jordan since I didn't want to scare her even more than she already was.

"We shouldn't have left you," said Ethan. "I'm sorry, honey."

"After we left you that night," said Ryder, and I could tell he was deep in thought, remembering. I didn't want to remember all the embarrassing things I yelled at him about. I wanted to forget and start over. "It was hard to let go and forget about you, knowing you were in danger. I shouldn't have allowed myself to walk out that door."

"Don't feel bad because if you didn't, I would've *really* flipped out," I said. "I didn't want to see reason after what you did to me."

Tempers were high that night, and there was no way I was going to let the bodyguards stay in my house after getting spanked by them.

"I missed you, Lacy, more than I thought I would," said Ryder, flipping over onto his side. I felt his dark gaze eating me up with his intense look. My heart was palpitating like crazy right now. I turned to look at him, locking gazes with the guard who stole my heart out of nowhere.

"Ryder," I said, my heart beating fast and hard in my chest. Tears pricked my eyes. "I missed you too. And you too, Ethan."

Ethan kissed my shoulder, his lips warming my skin. In turn,

Ryder leaned in, grasped my chin, and kissed me full on the lips. My eyes fluttered closed while we kissed on the bed like no tomorrow.

I missed him so much.

His leathery scent, in combination with his cologne, smelled so freaking addictive to me. His fingers on my chin were firm but not demanding. He didn't want to scare me, and I was free to break the kiss anytime, but I didn't want to.

After a few minutes, we pulled back at the same time, and I smiled shyly, my gaze resting on his chest. The intense look he was giving me was causing endless flutters in my belly, which traveled down my pussy.

"That was nice," he said.

"Yes," I said breathlessly.

Ethan placed his fingers on my chin, and I turned my head to face him next. His lips were sensual and plump as we kissed.

I was so sleepy that it felt like a dreamy sensation as I closed my eyes and kissed him back. His beard brushed my neck as our kiss intensified. His tongue pushed inside my mouth, roaming and exploring. I met his tongue with mine, also tasting him. I was getting hornier with every passing minute, and I grew more embarrassed by my smell as it got stronger in the room. This feeling wasn't at all like last night.

My body didn't respond this strongly to Jordan at all. Not even close.

This was a different feeling as I took in their kisses. Ethan's eyes were also closed by the time we were done kissing.

Both of their hands roamed down my body under the sheets, touching and exploring. I touched their chests as they untied their bathrobes. Their warm skin, sliding over mine, caused my heart to skip a beat. The heat rising under the sheets made me drunk off their scents.

"So fucking beautiful," said Ryder as he cupped my left breast. He kissed my breast, and Ethan did the same with my right one. They were both kissing and sucking on my nipples in unison.

171

Flurries of desire rippled through my belly.

Their hot mouths and rough tongues embracing my nipples caused me to desperately grasp their hair.

I moaned as Ryder looked straight up at me as he sucked on my nipple. I felt the tip of his tongue flicking my hardened bud back and forth, each flick sending electric shocks straight to my pussy.

"Oh god, we should stop before I end up pregnant," I said. "I'm not taking the suppressants."

With a groan, they both pulled away from my breasts. I knew it was hard to stop, and I was seriously considering just letting go and getting knotted, but I couldn't. Not yet anyway.

"You're like a delicious dessert waiting to be devoured," said Ryder, his hand rubbing my stomach. "Every part of your body is like a present waiting to be caressed."

"Fuck," said Ethan, rubbing his exposed penis, which was hard and thick. "I need to take care of this then, if you don't mind."

I licked my lips.

"I can help you take care of that," I said, and he looked at me with a feral look in his gaze. The same look he had given me during my bath.

"Oh, will ya'?" he asked gruffly, watching me with amusement. He pulled the sheets off. Then he knelt over me, placing each of his thighs on either side of my head, his cock swinging like a pendulum above my face. "Is this scaring you, sweetheart?"

"Doesn't scare me," I said, clenching my thighs together. Trying to control my own arousal. If we couldn't have sex, I might as well please the men who were here to protect and guard me.

Ryder was watching me silently as he gripped his own cock, and that only made me even hornier that he was watching.

Thirty

RYDER

While Lacy was too preoccupied with Ethan's cock in her mouth, I gradually shifted above her. I kissed her belly button, drinking in her deliciously sweet scent the closer I got to her pussy. I needed to taste her pussy, even if it was for a moment, our dangerous mission tomorrow. Anything could go wrong, and I could lose her again.

I couldn't lose her again. And it would take a hundred alphas to pry me from her.

I kissed her inner thighs, watching as she took Ethan's cock like the naughty omega she secretly was. It felt good to be the one to take her virginity, and I would be the only alpha who'd have her beside my pack.

The thought of Jordan torturing her last night killed me, and the despair in her voice was all too real.

I watched for a few minutes, getting hornier when her mouth was full with cock like that.

I needed her lips around my cock again.

"I'm going to taste your little pussy," I warned her, and she spread her legs wide in response.

Fuck.

Her pussy was covered in slick and dripping for me. Her lips

173

were bright pink as I spread her open with two fingers. Her cute ginger scent wafted to me, and I couldn't wait any longer. Holding her thighs open, I licked her pussy lips first. One lip at a time. She wiggled and squirmed, trying to force my tongue to go inside her.

"Patience, kitty," I crooned, holding her right pussy lip captive between my lips as I sucked her juices. I craved to shove my tongue deep inside her pussy, but I needed to taste every single drop of honey from her first. After I sucked off the right side of her pussy, I sucked her left folds into my mouth.

The taste of her was splendid. Like nothing I've ever tasted before. Her natural sweet odor mixed with an undertone of her omega perfume.

"Ugh," she called out, but her voice was muffled entirely by Ethan's thick cock shoved down her throat. I massaged her thighs to open up wider for me. Then I saw her pink clit peeking out.

I circled the tip of my tongue over her clitoris, enjoying how she shyly flinched, trying to hold it back from me. Her clit shuddered as I furiously lapped up the slick dripping from her center. Her pussy was warmer than usual, and concern flooded my mind. Could she be nearing her heat? Playing with her pussy like this would bring on her heat full force. *But wouldn't we have a few days before that happened?*

Pushing that thought out of my mind, I was desperate to spread her with my tongue. And also knot her if she wanted me to.

Pressing my finger inside her pussy, I sucked and licked her clitoris until she cried out again.

She was close.

Her thighs were beginning to shake, so I instead removed my finger from her pussy and shoved my thick tongue inside her hole. Her pussy squelched with every thrust of my tongue.

"I can hear your happy pussy," Ethan said to her.

"Mhmm," she moaned while Ethan knelt above her. His knees were on either side of her face as he jammed his cock into her mouth. She grabbed his ass cheeks, her nails digging into his skin while I pounded into her with my tongue. She was close to the edge, and I was going to give it all I got.

Using my thumb, I rubbed her peeking clit over and over. Adding pressure with every thrust of my tongue. I licked until her thighs started to shake uncontrollably, and her cries mingled with Ethan's groans as they both came.

I lapped up every drop from her fluttering pussy as she clenched around my tongue.

"I'm dying to knot inside your tight pussy," I said, and she tried to shut her legs in a panic. But I wasn't finished yet. I sucked her pussy while she drank down Ethan's liquid. He finally pulled his cock out of her mouth, which started to swell, and he collapsed next to her, massaging his dick. "Come for me again, Lacy."

"I can't!" she cried out.

"Yes, you can," I said, needing more of her.

Needing the taste of her on my tongue again.

I pressed my tongue deep inside her clenching pussy, wiggling it around for more of her precious liquid. Then I felt the well of her slick start to drip again on my tongue, and she moaned.

"Wait, the camera," she breathed, trying to reach around to pull the sheets up over my head. But I didn't want to be distracted as I felt her nectar hitting my tongue again. Let them see her legs spread for me. I hoped Jordan was watching every second of this. I lifted her legs up, spreading her wider, and she gasped at my boldness.

I plopped my tongue from her throbbing pussy.

"Fuck the cameras," I said, circling my tongue around her clit now. I pushed two fingers into her vagina while licking her clit repeatedly. "You had no problem masturbating in front of a camera, screaming my name. Isn't that right, kitten?"

"Oh god," she cried out, her pretty legs trembling again.

I quickly removed my fingers and sucked her pussy, drinking

her smooth honey slick down my throat. I sucked her until she stopped trembling with aftershocks of her orgasm.

"Fucking hell," I said while she was laying limply against the pillow. I pressed kisses against her trembling pussy, content with what she had given me so far. "Thank you, baby."

"You're welcome," she said shyly, still breathing hard with sweat dripping from her forehead. Her face was pink and so cute as she gazed at me in wonder. "I didn't think I could do that twice in a row."

"Now it's going to be a third time because we're going to switch," said Ethan and I smiled against her pussy as she gasped.

I stroked my hard dick and knelt over her head just like Ethan did while he took my place between her legs. He immediately started to lick her sensitive pussy while I positioned my cock directly over her. Her mouth was round with shock, and I took that opportunity to place the tip of my dick against her lips.

She shyly licked the tip of my cock, and I groaned at the feel of her sharp tongue flicking against the tip.

"Don't play with your food," I growled, and she smiled wickedly.

And that was all it took. Her disobedience turned me on every time.

I shoved my cock into her mouth, and she gasped at the thickness of it. "Did you forget my cock already? Let's rectify that." Her breaths came out in soft moans as I gripped the back of her head. Her warm mouth around my dick felt so fucking good as she sucked as hard as she could.

"Her pussy is fucking wet again," said Ethan, and I heard a long squelch while he played with her pussy.

"She's a naughty omega," I grunted as she bobbed her head, squeezing her lips tight around my cock. Her tongue swirled my tip, and my precum shot out into her mouth when she did that. My balls were tight as fuck, and I tried to hold back from coming too early.

I watched half my cock disappear into her mouth as she strained to take more of me in.

My breaths came out faster and shallower.

Our gaze was locked on each other as she bobbed her head frantically to please me. The movement of her tight lips and her swirling tongue on my dick made me grip her hair harder as I climaxed in her mouth. Stars clouded my vision as I released a stream into her mouth, which she quickly tried to swallow.

I pulled out before my cock knotted in her mouth, gripping it to keep the pressure on it as it swelled an angry purple. I dropped to the side, laying my head on the other half of her pillow.

My heart was hammering in my chest from the intensity of my orgasm.

"Good girl," I praised her, kissing her on the mouth as she moaned out her third orgasm while Ethan played with her pussy. Her warm breath against my lips felt so warm and comforting. She felt like home, and I couldn't explain it. "You did such a good job. I wish I could knot inside you."

"Thank you," she gasped, trying to come down for her own high. "We're crazy."

"Not crazy," I said, still tasting her scent on my tongue. "We missed each other, that's all."

"I must have missed you a lot," she said, rolling over to wrap her arms around me after Ethan was finished with her. Her heavy, warm breasts pressed against my chest, and I hugged her tightly to me. I enjoyed the sensation of her breasts heaving up and down with her fast breaths against me.

"We missed you more, sweetheart," I said. "You might not believe me when I say this, but I love you, Lacy."

"What?" she blinked, lifting her head sleepily.

"I love you," I repeated, my heart beating faster during my confession. "I don't expect you to say it back yet, but I wanted you to know that."

She nodded sleepily and closed her eyes. I knew she loved us too, but she wasn't ready to say it, and I wasn't going to rush her.

The tiny bit of doubt saddened me that she might not love me since I was just a bodyguard and she was a popular, beautiful singer.

Her soft snores soon sounded in the room, and her eyes closed.

"Stop worrying, Ryder," said Ethan, who could see the range of emotions cross my face as we watched her sleep in my arms, satisfied and content.

"How do you know I'm worrying?"

"She loves us, whether she's ready to admit it or not," said Ethan. "The way she holds onto you shows that she trusts you. The way her eyes light up when she sees us shows us her true feelings. Her feelings are crystal clear, but she's stubborn too."

I kissed Lacy on the forehead and smiled.

"You may be right, brother."

Thirty-One

LACY

The next morning, I was awake, but I kept my eyes closed. I allowed myself to remember everything from last night, unlike the night before with Jordan, which I blocked out. Ethan was still sleeping beside me, and I was excited to wake up between them.

Opening my eyes, I looked over at Ryder since Ethan was snoring. He was already awake and watching me with a quiet smile. The clock behind him on the wall said eight a.m.

"You were smiling when you were sleeping," he muttered, kissing me on the forehead. The kiss was tender and full of care, making my heart swell.

"I was remembering last night," I said, blushing. "How long were you watching me?"

"Long enough, kitten," he said, kissing me. It was a sleepy, good morning kiss that reminded me of our intimate night together. I wondered how it would feel to wake up to this every day.

The kiss was full of love, and I suddenly remembered his admission of love. My face was burning as I slowly broke the kiss.

"I need to wash up," I whispered, and Ethan let out a particularly louder snore that made us smile. When I got out of bed, rolling over Ryder's hairy muscular thighs, I felt slightly light-headed and grabbed the dresser for balance.

Ryder grasped my hip and looked at me in concern.

"Are you okay?" he asked.

"Yes," I said, rubbing my forehead. "Just a little light-headed. I must have moved too fast, and we did so much last night."

"You're right," he said, spanking me on my bare ass. I looked at him disapprovingly, and he grinned devilishly at me. But as I walked to the bathroom, I felt a sharp pain shooting down my belly to my pussy so I hurried into the bathroom and closed the door.

What was this pain?

I took deep breaths, waiting for it to pass. Maybe a warm shower would help. As the water washed over me, I held onto the shower door handle and flinched through the pain in my belly. I'd never felt this kind of pain before, and I started to wonder.

No, it couldn't be. I refused to dwell on it.

I straightened up, trying to ignore the pain as I rubbed the loofah around my body. A sharp tightening around my abdomen caused me to cry out and drop the loofah. I heard the bathroom door open and saw Ryder's blurry outline standing in front of the glass door. I held onto the handle, out of breath from the pain, my forehead pressed against the glass, fogging up from the steam of the shower.

"Are you okay in there?" asked Ryder.

"Yes," I moaned, not wanting him to know I was in heat.

"You don't sound well," he said. "I'm going to open the door, Lacy."

I lifted my head and shuffled backward, clutching my middle. Waves of fresh pain coursed through me, getting worse by the minute. When the band around my stomach tightened, my pussy would clench harder each time.

"Fuck," I cried out, holding his strong arm for balance as I hunched over.

"We'll take care of you, honey," Ryder said, quickly shutting off the water with his other hand while he let me use his arm for balance. He wrapped a towel around my shoulders and walked me to the bedroom. Upon seeing me, Ethan got up from the bed in alarm and rushed over to help, bringing me a dress.

"Is she in heat already?" asked Ethan.

"She is," said Ryder. "We need to get the hell out of here before anyone finds out. They'll take her instantly. She's in prime condition to be mated and bred."

Every step made the pain in my belly worse.

The feeling in my pussy wasn't painful like my belly, but the clenching showed me how important a knot was right now. In my gut, I knew a knot would help stop the pain. I cried out in agony, trying to sit on the bed.

"How the hell am I going to walk?" I said as Ethan helped pull the dress over me. Ryder was wrapping the black bathrobe around his body, tying up the rope, and Ethan followed suit.

"We need to take you out for a walk, and you have to pretend everything is fine," said Ryder. "I know it's a hard ask because I have no idea what kind of pain you're going through and..."

He stopped mid-sentence when the bedroom door burst open.

Startled by the crash of the door, I looked up, seeing Jordan and the alpha security barge right in. My heart raced as Ethan quickly scooped me up in his arms, inching towards the high window.

"We know who you are," Jordan hissed evilly with a white bandage over his nose. "I knew who the fuck you guys were, and I finally decided to tell them today."

"Oh really?" said Ryder. "We're here to breed omegas, just like you."

"Lies, lies," said Jordan as the security caved around us. "They know already. Hand us the omega, and we'll deal with you separately. Unless you want her hurt?"

I didn't notice Ryder standing at the window, and I started worrying. *Were they planning to freaking jump?* We were so high up that it would be dangerous. Before I knew it, Ethan and Ryder looked at each other, silently communicating.

At the same time, they smashed the window with their elbows. Glass shattered everywhere as Jordan charged at us.

"Hold onto my neck," ordered Ethan, flipping me onto his back, and I quickly grasped his neck as he jumped out the window. Time seemed to go by slowly as the air rushed around my face. I screamed as he shifted into his werewolf form in midair, landing on the sand seamlessly on his paws. I held onto his neck for dear life as he raced across the sand.

Shouts and gunshots rang through the air.

Ethan collapsed mid-run, and I was suddenly thrown into the air onto the sand. We were several feet apart while he and Ryder tried to fight off the guards. Shouts, grunts, and gunshots were all I heard.

Jordan approached me with glowing eyes as he climbed over my body. I held my belly as waves of pain held me captive.

I couldn't move, and he knew it.

"You're in heat, Pinkie," he said. Using the pet name I hated. "It's finally time, and you're in heat. You know I've been waiting for this a *long* time. It's going to turn me on so much to knot you while you try to fight me off."

"Get the fuck off her," shouted a deep voice.

My neck twisted so fast to look that it almost broke. Lucas arrived, carrying a huge gun between his hands. Cooper also rushed to help Ryder and Ethan.

"She's mine," snarled Jordan. Before he could pull out his own gun, Lucas had pressed the point of his gun to Jordan's forehead.

"Don't even try," said Lucas.

"Kill me then since you so badly want to," said Jordan, sneering.

When I looked at Lucas, all I saw was stone-cold rage in his eyes, and he shot Jordan without hesitation. I clapped a hand to

CRAVED BY THE PACK

my mouth in shock as I watched Jordan's body flop to the ground.

He lay next to me, eyes glassy and open. He was dead. An ex-boyfriend of mine, who I actually dated, was gone.

And I was relieved.

"Come on, beautiful," said Lucas, lifting me off the sand and into his arms.

I quickly looked around for Ethan and Ryder, but they were trying to hold back the guards from us, snapping at their legs and throwing them in the air. A few guards had shifted into their werewolf forms, biting Ryder. Lucas ran with me in his arms towards their armored van, and Adrian was waiting in front of it with a rifle.

I watched Cooper carefully take aim, shooting the werewolves who were biting into the bleeding Ryder.

"We can't leave them!" I shouted.

"They'll join us, don't you worry," said Lucas, plopping me into the van with Adrian's help. "Get her inside, now."

Adrian lifted me into the van, and Lucas went around the driver's side, revving up the engine. The back part of the van was a huge empty space where the men just sat on the floor with no seats. It was one enormous cavern that smelled like chips and alpha pheromones.

My pussy clenched painfully at their scents, reminding me that I needed a knot.

Ethan came into the van first, his werewolf form covered in red fur, which was matted and bloodied. He crawled up into the van with Adrian's help. Ethan grunted in pain as he shifted back into alpha form. His fur began to retract, revealing his skin. His right shoulder was completely bloodied, and I realized he had been shot.

"Oh my god, you're hurt," I groaned out from my pain. I was curled in pain in the corner, watching as Cooper and Ryder flew into the van next.

"Drive!" shouted Adrian. "Go, go, go!"

Lucas pumped the gas, driving a hundred miles per hour through the sand. Adrian slid the huge door shut to the sound of gunshots pinging off the metal of the door. I was shocked at how much it could withstand as gunshots continually rained down on it until we were finally out of the compound.

Everyone was breathing hard, looking at each other in wonder. We did it.

We finally escaped.

"We got to get you guys into a hospital right away," said Adrian, wrapping up Ryder's wounds. Ryder's leg had a huge gash that I could see through to the bone. Cooper pressed Ethan's shoulder with a rag, staunching the bleeding as he winced in pain. Ryder and Ethan were completely naked when they shifted back —broken and bloodied.

"Fuck," said Ryder when Adrian accidentally cut into his wound with the cloth.

"Sorry, man," said Adrian.

"Olivia," I said, shutting my eyes tight. "We completely left her behind."

I couldn't believe we fucking left her there.

"There's nothing we can do about it right now," grunted Ryder through his pain.

"We can't just leave her there!" I shouted. "She's going to suffer."

"Lacy, calm down," said Adrian, trying to pat my arm once he helped wrap up his wound. "We'll tell the proper authorities about this place to get it shut down. Lacy, what's wrong?"

"I'm in heat," I said, still upset that Olivia was stuck at the camp while I was able to escape.

I rested my head against one of the four walls of the van, hating this feeling. I vowed I would try everything in my power to help her. I would use my celebrity platform to help, and no one would stop me.

"You're in heat?" asked Adrian in shock, placing his hand on my shoulder.

"I'm taking you guys to the hospital," said Lucas. "Adrian, take care of Lacy. She needs a knot immediately."

"What? No," I said, crawling away from him. The pain was intense, but if I breathed through it, I could handle it. "I'm going to wait until you can take me to my house so I can take the heat suppressant pills."

"That's not how it works, honey," said Adrian, coming closer to me. "It would take weeks for it to take effect."

Thirty-Two

LACY

Stabbing pain gripped my belly as I huddled in the corner, grabbing Adrian's arm for balance as Lucas drove crazily down the road.

I didn't want a baby. I had everything I wanted in my life right now.

"No," I gasped out. "I can't have a baby right now."

"Lacy, I love you," said Ryder while he winced in pain. He watched me with one eye open as he lay limply in his spot. Cooper still held the rag to his shoulder. "I don't want to see you in pain."

"I know, but...," I said, knowing they weren't bad alphas. "I have everything all set up perfectly in my life right now."

"We all feel like that sometimes," said Adrian, gently touching my knee. I was still wearing the dress that Ethan helped me put on, and there was no way I was taking it off. "Didn't you ever see yourself being with a pack one day?"

"I mean, I have," I said. "But we need to take care of Ethan and Ryder first. They're about to die."

"Knot her, Adrian," said Ryder, who completely passed out by now, laying on the floor of the van.

"Oh no," I moaned, crawling to Ryder. He had risked his life for me. I touched the stubble of beard on his jaw. "Ryder, please stay with us."

Cooper pressed a hand to his chest. "He's still alive. He passed out, but the elements of his alpha blood will help him through this."

"It's two hours to the nearest hospital," said Lucas, speeding across empty streets and roads.

We were still so far away from civilization. Ethan was in bad shape, with one leg out and wrapped in white t-shirts, but he hadn't gone unconscious yet. Worry pooled in my soul while the pain from my heat kept me hunched over. Tears streamed down my face. It was impossible to think I'd last through my heat until I got home.

Cooper grasped my hand, forcing me to look at him.

"Lacy," he said. "Why won't you let us help you? I will stand by your side no matter what happens. I will help you raise the child."

I shook my head frantically, more tears falling to the floor.

"I *do* want to trust you," I said, crying, pulling his hand to my heart. "I want to trust you all so bad, but what if you hurt me in the end? What if you decide you don't want me anymore?"

Adrian was immediately at my other side, rubbing my back.

"We're not like your ex," said Adrian. "Like the psychopath that you fell in love with."

"If I ever lost you, I would hunt for you to the ends of the earth," said Cooper, locking eyes with me. He looked at me with such intensity that it made my heart pause. My pussy pulsed and quivered with need. I don't know if it was because he played music like myself, but he had that personality that I leaned into. His calm, quiet demeanor helped me stay calm. "Let Adrian knot you. I can't knot you since I'm a delta. I'll take care of Ryder and make sure he doesn't die in the middle of the trip."

It was true. The pack had enough to be worried about right now.

Taking a deep breath, I turned to Adrian, and he wiped my

tears with his thumb. His light touch sent desire rippling through me. A want for him to be deep inside me took over any other thought as he kissed me.

While we kissed, he carried me back into my corner. I touched his curly black hair, pushing it away from his eyes. He slowly lifted the edge of my dress, revealing my clenched thighs.

The pain was getting more intolerable by the minute.

I allowed Adrian to part my legs. Adrian rubbed my thighs, slowly pushing them apart further as I lay on my back.

"I'm sorry, it's the pain," I whispered.

"It's okay beautiful," he said, gazing at my heated slit. "All the pain will go away very soon, okay baby?"

"Okay," I said, watching as he unbuckled his belt and shed his pants. My heart hammered in my chest as he settled between my legs, his cock angry and hard. "Oh, your big Adrian."

"Do you think you can take this big cock inside of you?" he asked, rubbing the tip against my slick pussy.

Oh god, I wanted him so deep inside until it hurt.

"Yes," I cried out when I felt him tease my pussy lips open with his cock. He penetrated me, and I gasped at how it stretched me. It felt so deliciously good, and now I started to believe it when omegas claimed how much they needed knots during their heats.

"*Fuck yes*," groaned Adrian as he slid all the way inside due to my slick. "Such a tight beautiful pussy."

I gripped his arms as he thrust into me.

"Yes, harder," I begged.

Then he savagely thrust into me, and I screamed with pleasure as his cock stretched me out. His thick cock pulsed angrily inside me while he pulled back and thrust back in. Every thrust felt like he was nailing his penis inside me.

"You're mine, Lacy," he said, eyes dark with rut and lust. "Your pussy belongs to this pack only. Got it?"

I nodded in response.

"Answer me, baby," he said, pounding into me while the van shook over the dirt roads.

"Yes," I gasped when he pushed in extra hard so I could understand.

"Yes, what?"

"My pussy belongs to you and the pack," I shuddered as I clenched around his cock. The pain in my belly subsided with my orgasm, and my pussy clenched more furiously around him.

"Fuck," he rasped out as he climaxed, spilling hot spurts of semen inside of me. My pussy throbbed and clenched with after-shocks. And when his dick finally swelled within me, the pain slowly receded. My body was now satisfied and complete with his knot. He leaned down, kissing me on the lips.

"I feel better now," I said as we held each other. I was happy it was Adrian who knotted me since we already had so much chemistry and flirted constantly before this horrible kidnapping.

"I told you, baby," said Adrian, pushing back my sweat-strewn hair away from my face.

My dress was hitched up, showing our connected privates as he lay beside me. I could feel his knot pulsing inside me as he continued to release more semen. I wiggled my hips, but the knot was in me tight, swelling at the base of his penis.

"I'm worried about Ryder and Ethan," I said, looking over at them as Cooper went back and forth between them, pouring water onto their faces and taking care of them while Adrian knotted me.

"They'll make it," said Adrian. "Just focus on your pleasure right now and my knot deep inside you."

"Okay," I sighed, rubbing his chest. "Thank you for knotting me."

"Don't ever thank me," said Adrian. "You are my priority and my only love. I'm glad no one else was able to breed you or mark you at that camp. The thought of that sickens me."

"You guys came just in time," I said. "I could've been trapped there and pregnant. Which is why I feel so upset we can't save Olivia."

"We were under gunfire," said Adrian. "Otherwise, things would've been different. Were you scared at the camp?"

I was surprised he cared how I felt during my time there.

"I was," I admitted. I couldn't forget the fear of Jordan coming into my room the second night, but the relief I felt when I saw Ryder instead was insurmountable. Nothing could replace the joy I felt last night. This pack brought me safety and happiness that I couldn't explain.

Thirty-Three

LACY

After Lucas dropped off Ryder and Ethan at the hospital, I was taken to a hotel nearby to take care of my heat. Cooper and Lucas surrounded me in the enormous bed while I was knotted to Adrian.

For the second time.

"How are you going to keep up with me?" I asked Adrian as he pet my pussy which was thankfully filled with his knot.

"After my knot goes down, Cooper or Lucas will take you next," said Adrian. "And then I'll take over again."

"Damn, we only have one alpha here. None of us can knot," said Cooper out loud while tracing my shoulder from the back. He was lying in bed naked next to me after I reassured him that it was fine for him to stay at the hospital. But he insisted on ensuring I was okay before he went back to the hospital to check on Ethan and Ryder.

"Go ahead, Cooper," said Lucas, nodding as he sat on the bed, observing my every move. "We're going to make sure we take care of our beautiful omega."

Adrian's knot began to gradually recede in size, letting me loose. At first, it was okay for a few minutes, and the pain was not so bad.

Then I felt the crushing pain again in my pelvis as the invisible band squeezed.

"I'm sorry, I need to recuperate," said Adrian, who saw me wince in pain. "Cooper, do your best, man."

Cooper climbed on top of me, his chiseled chest right before my eyes. It was a sight I couldn't get enough of. He was tan and seriously hot as hell. I wondered why he hadn't snagged an omega for the pack before me. He kissed me full on the mouth, and I kissed him back, urgently needing him inside even though he couldn't knot me.

"Are you ready, baby?" he asked against my lips.

"Please, Cooper," I whined, eager for him to be inside me already. This heat was so painful and something I was unprepared for. I clawed at his back as he plunged his cock deep inside me. It relieved some of the pain, but the tightening in my belly grew worse as he thrust inside of me. My body was waiting eagerly for his knot as he continued to thrust.

"Fuck, your pussy is clenching so hard, baby," said Cooper, his eyebrows furrowed. "I don't think it's enough without a knot."

I cried out when another stabbing pain shot through my belly.

"I'll take her ass," said Lucas, quickly positioning me onto my side. "I think it might help if there's some fullness there, too."

I was fearful of a whole dick inside of my ass, but at this point, slick was dripping from me, and I was desperate for some relief. Adrian was furiously pumping his cock as he watched us from the edge of the bed.

"This will take care of you until Adrian is ready," said Lucas, spreading my ass cheeks apart while Cooper continued to pump into my pussy. My breathing was accelerated as I waited for the knot that would never come.

I cried out again, with pain squeezing my body.

Lucas quickly fingered my ass hole with his finger, and I could feel his probing finger trying to push inside. Testing how ready I was.

"I'm so sorry, honey," said Cooper while a stream of his hot liquid spurted inside me.

"It's okay," I said, tears pricking my eyes at the lack of a knot. Lucas was probing my anus with his cock, and I cried out as he pushed the tip inside. I had no idea how that would help me until he showed me.

"Relax for me," said Lucas, his strong hand gripping my breast from behind as he plunged in. I cried out at the impact, but at the same time, any sort of fullness felt good. My pussy felt empty when Cooper finally pulled out, kissing me.

"Hurry, Adrian. I hate seeing her in pain," said Cooper.

"Dude, it's not easy to go again after one minute," said Adrian, pumping his cock. But I was relieved to see he was fully hard, at least. Lucas kissed my shoulder as he continued to fuck my ass, turning me onto my belly.

"Hey, it was longer than a minute for me," said Cooper, shaking his head as he got off the bed. "I'm going to check on Ryder and Ethan. We fucking need them to take care of our omega. We can't do it alone."

I gripped the hot, sweaty sheets as Lucas pumped my ass with his cock. The pressure of him on top of me forced my belly to stop contracting as much with the heat pains. The applied pressure he was adding was helping.

"Do you feel a little bit better, omega?" asked Lucas, pulling back and slamming into my stretching ass. "Your ass was made for me."

"It's my first time," I cried out.

"You're an omega, don't worry. You're fuckable from your ass and pussy," said Lucas, thrusting harder into me. I bit into the pillow, enjoying the way his cock curved. It wasn't painful, but it shocked me. "Is it hurting you, baby?"

"No," I cried out when he thrust inside me harder. "It's making me forget the pain in my pussy."

"Good," crooned Lucas, lightly biting my shoulder from behind and causing me to yelp at the stinging sensation. I glowed from deep within me. "You're *my* omega."

"Yes," I moaned as he finally thrust into me one last time, lifting my hips off the bed. My ass was hurting and sore when he pulled out, slapping my ass cheek.

"That was splendid," said Lucas. "Next, I'll put a baby inside that pussy, but Adrian will knot you now." He rubbed my ass cheeks and flopped onto his side, kissing my arm as Adrian settled over me from behind.

"I'm going to knot your little pussy again," said Adrian. "This time from behind. Got it?"

"Yes," I breathed, unable to wait any longer. This heat demanded things from me that made me shameless.

"On your knees," he said. I tried to get up, but my legs were still shaking after being taken so hard in the ass, so Adrian's strong hands came around, lifting me onto my knees.

"Thank you," I said as he kissed my ass cheeks.

"Your ass is dripping everywhere," he said. "I'm going to make your pussy drip just as equally. Let me spread your knees apart further."

I bowed my head as I waited in anticipation. My belly was clenching and releasing slick at a rapid pace, knowing that an alpha was nearby. The sweaty sheets twisted around me in a makeshift, messy nest. My ginger scent overwhelmed the room, and I was dying to shower after this.

Adrian pushed my legs apart with his knee while my elbows still touched the bed. I was as wide open as he wanted me to be.

"Please," I whined. He pressed his finger into my pussy and groaned in satisfaction at the amount of slick I'd produced while Lucas fucked my ass.

"Ahh," he said as he penetrated my pussy from behind.

It felt so deliciously good that I closed my eyes.

I wanted to absorb his thickness into me as much as possible while he was inside. He thrust into me with as much force as he could muster with a loud, squelching sound. Each thrust made the bed squeak and crash against the wall. I was worried the people in the next room might know an omega was in heat.

"Oh," I cried when he gripped my hair, pulling my head back. Oh gosh, Adrian had a secret side to him that I didn't know about. He was a pure wolf in bed. His other hand gripped the side of my hip while he rutted me thoroughly.

"Fuckin' good," growled Adrian. The rate of my breathing increased as I felt him hitting my g spot repeatedly.

"The neighbors might hear," I cried out.

"Let them fucking hear," said Adrian. "Let the whole world know you're mine."

"Oh, it feels so good," I moaned. Lucas quickly snaked a hand underneath my belly, rubbing my clitoris. The sensation mounted like a storm within me until I yelled out in pleasure.

Adrian still gripped my hair as he pumped me full.

He growled when he came inside me, slowly relaxing his hold on my hair, and I collapsed onto the bed. He laid on me from behind, kissing my shoulders and neck. We breathed hard for a few minutes while his dick knotted me tight against him. The feeling of his knot swelling inside me brought me instant relief, and I yawned.

Lucas was in the shower now, while Cooper had already left to check on Ryder and Ethan.

"So good," said Adrian. "I never helped an omega through a heat before."

"You're doing an amazing job," I said.

"Thank you," said Adrian, kissing my collarbone softly. "When will you call your parents and tell them you're okay?"

I thought about that one while during the ride here.

"I don't want them to know I'm in heat or anything," I said. "I'll call them as soon as my heat's over."

"Why?"

"It's just that...they've seen me have such control over my life," I explained. "I'd rather they not know about this."

I know my mom was worried senseless about me right now, but my family would want to see me right away. And I was a little embarrassed to be in heat after doing everything to prevent it.

"Understandable," said Adrian. "I admire how perfectly organized you are about everything. I'm the complete opposite."

"I know," I smiled, basking under his warmth in the bed. It was like our little nest since I couldn't be in my nesting room. I specifically decorated the room in my house for when I'd have a pack one day, but it ended up being useless.

Maybe for my next heat. *Oh god*, I couldn't believe I was already thinking about my next heat.

"I love you," Adrian muttered, kissing me until I slept.

~

I DIDN'T REALIZE I had fallen asleep until I groggily opened my eyes to a darkened room. Adrian's weight was no longer on top of me. The painful throbbing between my legs was what probably woke me up. I slowly turned onto my back, seeing a form lying next to me.

I looked to my right and saw Ryder smiling at me.

My heart leaped with joy. His shoulder was bandaged up, and he wore next to nothing, his cock pointing straight at the ceiling. He smelled like he was freshly showered, unlike myself, where I needed a bath badly. My scent was sickly sweet, overwhelming the room. I was scared of what they thought of me right now.

"Good morning, little omega," Ryder greeted, even though it was practically nighttime.

"You're back," I said gleefully, hugging him, and he winced. "Oh shit, sorry. Where's Ethan?"

I looked around and saw Ethan sitting around the table, eating with the others. He blew me a kiss and winked at me.

"Don't worry. I'm coming for you, baby. After Ryder is through with you," said Ethan. His leg was wrapped in gauze, and

I wondered how he was going to knot me, but I'd let him determine that.

I turned my attention back to Ryder and kissed him on the lips. He kissed me back, his tongue into my mouth as he groaned.

"I couldn't wait to see you again," he muttered.

"Are you sure you're okay enough for...?"

"Damn sure," said Ryder, pulling me on top of him in one swift move.

"Wait, I want to shower real quick," I said.

"That can wait," he said, guiding my pussy over his huge cock with intensity in his gaze. My breathing quickened as his cock stretched me further and further. "Oh fuck yes. Bounce on me, baby."

Using the strength from my thighs, I gripped his good arm as I lifted my lower half and grinding my pussy down onto his cock.

"Oh, Ryder," I hissed, enjoying how his length speared into me.

I felt like I was still in a dream as I rode him. I bounced up and down his impossible pulsing cock.

"Feels so fucking good. Continue," he said huskily, guiding me.

I was riding the pack leader of this group, and the thought turned me on so much I quivered around his cock. As I trembled and lost strength from my orgasm, he gripped my hips and lifted me up and down like a toy.

He pressed me down hard over his cock, keeping me there while his cock exploded inside me. His eyes were dark with lust as he pumped his liquid into me. His member soon swelled inside me, and I laid on his chest in relief from the heat pains.

"Good girl," he said, squeezing my ass cheeks as I relaxed on his body. "My cock can't get enough of you. Every minute in the hospital was a waste of time until I yelled at the damn doctor to discharge me."

"I can't get enough of you either," I said. "I love you, Ryder."

His eyes widened as I lifted my head to look at his reaction.

There was something else there. A range of emotions was going through him as his eyes sparkled with unshed tears. I was surprised at the amount of emotion my words elicited in him.

"You have no idea how much those words mean to me," he said. "I'm lucky to have found you, my love."

"I'm luckier," I said. I never felt so sure in my life until this moment while he was knotted inside me. It was a brand new feeling I never felt before in my life. A feeling I didn't want to end. I bit him lightly on the shoulder, and he growled.

"You're mine," he said, sinking his teeth into my shoulder in turn. I cried out at the pain while the rest of the men joined me in bed- kissing every part of me now that their pack leader had marked me as their omega. "You're *our* omega."

"Our omega," the men breathed in unison, hot breaths on my face, nipples, thighs and ass. Every inch of me was covered. I was scared they would all bite me at once, but they didn't.

With that, I relaxed against his chest, absorbing all the love the pack had to give me tonight and forever.

Thirty-Four

LACY

The morning my heat ended, I was taking a warm shower at the hotel- excited to go home and see my family. Last night, I had lingering after-effects of a sore pussy from the intense knotting from my alphas. Even this morning, I felt it as I carefully washed between my legs with the sponge.

It was a pleasant ache, nothing like the days of heat pangs I went through. That's when I knew I was feeling better and out of heat.

When I woke up this morning, I called my mom and told her I was fine. She squealed and yelled excitedly that I wasn't dead, making sure my fathers could hear. She was upset to hear about Olivia, and it was hard for me to tell them that she was still trapped at the OBC. But they were excited to see me regardless, and she said they'd be waiting at my house today. I smiled, remembering the conversation as I stood under the water, letting it soak my hair.

I felt a presence outside the shower door and saw a shadow standing there. My heart jumped after being stalked for weeks, but it was Ethan when he slid the glass door open. He stood there in all his naked glory, his cock erect as he gazed at me.

"You ran away from us this morning," he growled, rubbing his beard. "We always shower together, my love."

"Oops, I'm sorry," I giggled when he shoved himself into the shower with me, shutting the glass door behind us. I was locked in the shower with this older alpha who couldn't get enough of me. And who I couldn't get enough of either.

He pulled me towards him, kissing me hard on my wet lips with the shower water pouring over us. I plastered my wet breasts against his chest, and his dick pressed against my stomach, pulsing and throbbing. I knew what he wanted instantly, and he wasn't going to wait.

"I'm going to knot your pussy, lovely," he said, lifting my right leg over his shoulder. My breaths came out in gasps from arousal as he pressed his dick against my pussy entrance. "You're so wet for me."

"It's from the water," I teased, and he gripped my ass cheek warningly.

"You're wet because I'm in here with you," he growled, nipping my ear, and I yelped. My pussy clenched in anticipation, eager for him to be inside me already. But he lengthened the torture by slowly rubbing his dick in circles around my pussy. Slick, mixed with water, seeped out of me as I tried to hump him, but his grip on my ass cheek stopped me from taking him in too fast.

With my right leg up, he thrust inside me in one lightning move, and I cried out in pleasure.

He smiled devilishly as he gazed at me.

"Are you trying to punish me?" I breathed, touching his wet beard.

"No, I just couldn't wait to sink into your tight warm pussy," he grunted as he thrust into me. "I had a morning dream I was knotting you, and imagine my disappointment upon waking up."

Each thrust made my eyes roll back in my head, stretching me each time. He held my ass tightly so I didn't fall, but his finger slipped between my ass cheeks.

I breathed in anticipation.

Then he pushed his finger into my ass, the pleasurable burning sensation intensifying the more he pushed his finger inside my butt. His dick pulsed inside me as he pounded in harder and harder, my legs shaking. I felt my stomach tighten more and more with intense pleasure. His rugged face was inches from mine, contorted in pleasure as he watched my face for any signs of discomfort, but I was enjoying this more than he knew.

"You're so beautiful every time I pump you with my cock," he said. "You can't help but open your little mouth."

I didn't realize I was moaning until he pressed his tongue into my mouth. I closed my eyes, enjoying the sensation of his finger in my ass and his cock inside my pussy. I moaned even louder when I felt the crescendo of pleasure intensify. I came over onto cock, shattering around him as he drank my moans.

"Oh Ethan, that was so good..." I said as he grunted out his own pleasure. The warmth of his cock inside me felt so good as he slid to the floor of the bath, pulling me to sit on top of him with my legs around his waist. The showers were huge in this hotel, to probably accommodate an omega and her alphas.

He knotted inside me while the water washed over us, soaking us together.

"I love fucking you in the shower," he said. "I'm never allowing you to masturbate with your vibrator ever."

"Wait, how did you know...?"

"Did you think I didn't notice the damn toy sitting on the shelf of your bathtub?" he asked, pulling me close and kissing me again on the mouth. I pulled back, my face burning with embarrassment.

"You weren't supposed to go into my bathroom," I said.

"It was for investigative purposes," he said, rubbing his teeth against my neck. I braced myself, knowing what was coming next. He bit me, a sharp nick, and I whined against him as he rubbed my back. "I love you little omega."

"That one hurt," I said, snuggling against his wet, hairy chest. "But I love you too, my alpha."

"Hmm, I like the sound of that," he said, squeezing my butt against his knot as I wiggled over him in contentment. His knot was snug and deep inside me as we sat hugging each other, waiting for it to release us.

~

A COUPLE OF HOURS LATER, I was nearly jumping out of my seat when we drove up to my house. The beautiful house that I worked so hard for. The sight of my ornate gate made the feeling of coziness settle inside me. My stalker, who was part of a psychotic group, was finally dead, and the nightmare was finally behind me. But the sadness of leaving Olivia behind loomed over me, and it would follow me until she was safe.

At the sight of my mother standing at the door to my home, I smiled.

"She's been waiting for you," said Adrian, squeezing my waist.

"I know," I said, quickly hopping out of the van.

My clean cornflower blue dress swung around me as I ran to hug my mother. Her long red hair was identical to mine as it flowed in the wind.

"My baby," she cried, hugging me tightly. "I'm so sorry. I never thought this would happen…"

"It's not your fault," I said, my voice muffled against her ample chest. She smelled like onions and food, probably cooking all day for our arrival. Gabe pulled me out of her arms and gave me a large hug. He rubbed my hair, messing up my bun.

"Gabe!" I screamed at him, and he chuckled, his arms at his side now.

"I was scared we lost you," he said, and I could hear the trembling emotion in his voice. I was his baby sister, and I knew he was worried sick. "Welcome home, sis."

"Thanks, Gabe," I said, pinching his cheek, and he scowled. "Don't worry now, I'm home and safe."

Everyone had come out of the house to see me, and I was surprised to see Jade there along with my nephew, Manny.

"I'm so glad you're safe," said my aunt Jade, looking at me with tears in her eyes. "You're like a daughter to me, as you know. Please tell me how Olivia is doing, every detail."

"Of course," I said soberly. It was a horrible thing to come back safe and sound without Olivia. I felt intensely guilty like never before. We really should've tried harder.

We were all sitting around my dining table as I relayed everything that happened to me over the past week. I glossed over the part about me going into heat, but Manny guessed it instantly.

"Did you mate with your bodyguards?" he asked, digging into the chicken my mother and Jade had baked. "You smell like them."

"I...yes," I said meekly. I wanted to tell them when I was ready, but my mother smiled widely, looking back and forth between Ryder and me.

"You finally found your true pack of love," she said. "Your fathers will see you later, and I hope they approve of these wonderful bodyguards who went to hell and back for you."

"I hope so, too," I said. My dad, Alex, who was the pack leader, was hard to impress. But my dad, Jack, who was second-in-charge, would usually intercede for me. Jack was Jade's brother. Having seven dads with different opinions was sometimes a nuisance, and I wished my life was simpler.

"I'm sorry we couldn't save your daughter," Ryder addressed my aunt.

"From what Lacy had said," said Jade. "It sounded next to impossible at that time. I understand. Manny is trying to convince the Royal Pack to go after them since he's their prince. But the government is reluctant to go after their own kind."

"For right now, Olivia is doing okay," I said, trying to soothe her a little. "Omegas are pampered over there. Lots of massages and food."

"What if Olivia goes into heat at that place?" asked Manny with dread. His question made everyone stop chattering excitedly about my arrival. It was a looming cloud that hung over us, not something that I could forget easily.

"If the authorities don't do anything after the information you gave them, we will have to step in," said Ryder. "I'll give you the exact location of the camp so you can let King Armon know."

For the rest of that day, I talked with my mother and Gabe, catching up. We sat in the living room, away from the rest, and we talked about everything, including my attraction to my body-guards. Aunt Jade had left early, and Manny was discussing things with my pack.

"They better find Olivia," said my mom, leaning against the couch arm with a hand on her forehead. "I almost lost my mind when I saw you on the news."

"I know, Mom," I said.

"Mom didn't sleep, and our dads had to force her to eat," said Gabe.

"Oh my god, Mom," I said.

"It's okay now, baby," she said, sighing and rubbing her face. She had new wrinkles on her face that I hadn't seen before, and I hoped it wasn't from me being kidnapped. "The government needs to do something about it, and I think you need cameras everywhere."

"I know, Ryder won't let that one go," I said.

"Listen to your pack," said Mom. "They will protect you to the ends of the earth for you. I believe that."

"I know," I said, my heart warming.

Thirty-Five

LACY

The next day- I woke up to Ryder kissing me on the cheek. We had all collapsed in my nesting room with all the feathers from the pillows still everywhere once everyone was gone. I curled up into the blankets tighter, trying to ignore him.

"Baby, it's in the afternoon," he whispered, tickling me with a feather on my cheek.

"That's fine, we just got home," I mumbled, turning my head to the other side, but he wrapped an arm around me, hugging me.

I was exhausted after my heat and everything I went through. My body felt heavy, and my legs felt like logs. Ryder's arm around me made everything even more cozy, and I fell asleep again.

Snoring awake, I opened my eyes- horrified to find myself snoring. Something was going on between my legs, a rough tongue licking my clit. I looked down to see a smiling Ryder staring at me with his head between my legs.

"Are you finally awake, love?"

"Oh my god," I groaned. "I am. But why are you licking my pussy? You know that's creepy, right?"

"I love you," he said simply.

"Ryder," I said, trying to move his head out of the way with a weak hand, but he didn't budge. My pussy throbbed, and that would probably explain the naughty dreams I've been having all morning. His tongue plunged inside me, and I moaned. "Ryder, I need...a shower."

But he didn't answer as he licked me repeatedly until I felt my belly clench. His grunts down there made me horny as fuck, as he pretty much ate breakfast from between my legs.

I clenched my thighs around his head, which didn't dislodge his tongue from my pussy.

He licked my clit in a back-and-forth motion as his finger plunged into my pussy next. My breathing quickened as I felt the familiar tightening sensation. I moaned as slick dripped from my pussy. I collapsed back against the giant cushion, my legs spread wide open as he licked me clean.

"So good," he said. "Thanks for feeding me."

"No problem," I said, blushing. He finally lifted his head from between my legs when he was done, squeezing my thighs. "Where's everyone else?"

"They're putting something together for you," he said lazily, kissing my thighs. "I need you to get ready for our big surprise."

"For?" I asked, my curiosity piqued now.

"It's a surprise," he said. "I'll go shower, but I want to see you downstairs, ready to go in a couple of hours."

I scrunched my eyebrows, confused out of my mind. I just woke up feeling like a ton of bricks, just got eaten out, and now he had some weird surprise.

I didn't trust him or whatever crazy plan he was thinking of.

"Listen, I'm used to a schedule and some order in my life," I said, panicking. "I have a job, remember?"

"Call them then," he said, standing up and stretching fully naked. I couldn't help but stare at his hard dick, prominent and big. I was surprised he didn't immediately knot me right away. He must be excited to show me the surprise- and no wonder he kept waking me up. "I promise after today, things will hopefully return to normal."

~

A FEW HOURS LATER, I sat in the limo beside Ryder while my driver Phil drove us. Phil was excited to see me, and he made sure to open the door for me when I showed up. He didn't show emotion, but I could see his enthusiasm by how fast he opened the door for me.

"Are you going to tell me now?" I asked, rubbing my hand on Ryder's thigh. He looked handsome wearing black jeans and a blue dress shirt. He was casually dressed, and I wondered if we weren't going to a fancy dinner like I imagined. I wore a ruffled pink skirt with a tight black top, long silver earrings, and a silver heart necklace. I dressed fancy today, expecting a nice dinner, so I started to get self-conscious as I sat there next to him.

He pulled my hand from his thigh, kissing my palm.

"Why do you want to know so badly? Do you hate surprises?"

"I don't like being caught off-guard," I whined.

"So you're a perfectionist," he said, kissing my neck and making my earring jangle. My neck heated at the contact, and he pulled away, smiling. "I can smell that you're getting aroused, little omega. Not yet."

"I want you," I said, clenching my thighs under the skirt. I was embarrassed that he had already sensed my need and desire for him.

"Tonight," he whispered in my ear, his arm around my waist, hugging me to him. "Tonight, you will get knotted and fucked by all of us. Are you ready for that?"

"Yes, I think so," I breathed, hoping Phil couldn't hear anything over the loud air conditioner.

~

WHEN WE FINALLY REACHED THE location of the surprise, I was shocked to see the evening sky lit up with lights. Ryder got out of the limo first and took my hand in his. There was a Ferris wheel and rides everywhere.

"Wait, did you take me to a carnival?" I asked, looking around in awe. I was always surrounded by fans and people- a place I usually avoided at all costs.

"Yes, baby," he said, looking at me while I drank in the sight. "And it's all yours for tonight."

"What?" I squealed excitedly, and he smiled. I looked back at the lights and display, my heart pounding excitedly. "Let's go, Ryder!"

I could see he was more excited than I was when we walked towards the front booth. Behind the booth sat Adrian with a smirk.

"Tickets, please," he said, holding his hand out. "Just kidding, kisses for entrance."

I leaned forward, pursing my lips, and he wrapped his hand behind my neck, kissing me sensually.

"God, I missed you this morning," he said, and I drank in his scent. His essence was all around me, and I smiled.

"I missed you too," I muttered against his lips.

"Let's have some fun," said Ryder, his hand still in mine. I grabbed Adrian's hand as well, and when I entered the park, I gasped when I saw my entire family there, along with Ben, Ty, and his wife. They were all dressed in ripped jeans and dark shirts.

"Hey guys," I said to my co-workers.

"It's awesome your pack was able to reserve this entire park!" said Ben.

"We're excited to see you again," said Ty, giving me a one-armed hug. "Glad to see you're okay."

"Thank you," I said. Every time someone mentioned it, I kept thinking back to Olivia. God, how I wished I could see her again. I'd give anything to see her one more time. "I'm glad to be back. I just got home last night."

Next, I talked to my dads, who were astonished to see Ryder

CRAVED BY THE PACK

and the rest of my men. My dad, Alex, clapped Ryder on the back, thanking him for saving me.

"You made a good choice there, daughter," Alex said to me.

"I thought you'd be mad or something," I said. "You always hated the boyfriends I'd bring home in the past."

"Because I knew who they were," he said. "Look what happened with your ex. It's a good thing your boyfriend killed him."

"Alright, Dad, never mind," I said, not wanting his opinion anymore on my dating life. But I was glad he at least approved of Ryder. After talking to my fathers, I decided to have some fun with my pack.

"Yes?" said Ethan, who was eating cotton candy.

"Let's go to the Ferris wheel," I said as they all surrounded me. They agreed wholeheartedly while I took a ton of pictures. I felt extra cute today, and I wanted pictures. It was an amazing feeling being high up in the air and seeing all my friends and family below us enjoying their day.

Cooper squeezed my hand, and Lucas kissed my shoulder. It was the best day of my life, but Olivia was still missing...

"What's wrong, baby?" said Cooper, who had been observing me the entire time.

"This was one of the best days in my life," I said. "But I feel guilty."

"Because?" asked Lucas.

"Olivia is still trapped in that hellhole," I said.

"I know," said Cooper. "They're looking for her, and they'll save every omega in there. There's nothing you can do now but wait."

I nodded, feeling reassured as I leaned against his shoulder. The ocean looked so beautiful from high up, and being in the same little space with my pack comforted me. I wished it could be like this forever.

After we got off the Ferris wheel, Ryder turned to me and

waved over for everyone to come over. I looked around, confused. My family and co-workers stood around us, smiling.

I wondered if Ryder was about to give a speech or something.

Under the glowing lights of the Ferris wheel, my bodyguards and I stood, their faces illuminated with affection and anticipation. The carnival's lively atmosphere surrounded us, but for that moment, it was as if time had slowed down, and it was just us.

"What's going on?" I asked softly. Then they moved away from me, walking backward and forming a circle around me.

I stood there confused and feeling dumb for a moment.

Then I saw the sand light up with the words, "Will you marry us?" in glowing, radiant letters under the night sky.

My breath caught in my throat, and my eyes filled with tears.

The men closed the circle, surrounding me instead with their intense energies around me. The two deltas and the three alphas all surrounded me, with only me in the reflection of their gazes.

Ryder knelt, his head bowed as he faced me, and I gasped. But right at that moment, the rain started to come down, drenching everyone on the beach. The rain was still coming down, but Ryder did not get up from the ground. I was breathing so fast, not from the rain but from my nerves.

Was he really about to propose to me?

"Damn it," said Ryder, and I smiled at him. "It's not supposed to rain, but I can't let another day go by without asking you this question."

I placed a hand on my chest as he opened a small box in his hand.

"Oh," I gasped at the glittering ring inside.

"On behalf of my pack," said Ryder. "As the leader of my pack, I have sought permission from each of your fathers, who have granted me their approval. My beautiful Lacy, you've dropped into our lives in the most unexpected way, and we've all gotten to love you through it all. Will you do us the honor of marrying me, Ethan, Lucas, Cooper, and Adrian?"

It was an actual marriage proposal. And I never expected it to happen right now.

Panic stirred within me, but the feelings of excitement overrode it. I was going to have a pack just for me. A dream that I believed gone long ago.

"Yes," I said, smiling and crying in the rain. He slid the beautiful ruby ring studded with gold onto my finger and stood back up. He cradled my head and kissed me on the lips to the clapping and cheers of everyone around us. "I can't wait for our wedding."

"We're getting married right now," said Ryder with a grin.

Suddenly, I looked up and saw a group of workers hurry a fixture of a tall arch towards us, and suddenly, I was standing underneath an arch with flowers hanging down.

"What?" I said, laughing. I couldn't believe my pack had done all this. I wanted to laugh and cry at the same time. I was so touched, and my heart had grown ten sizes right about now. I couldn't help laughing when I saw a clown rushing to us with a book in his hand. "Is he officiating?"

"Yes," said Ryder.

Someone had stuck a tiara with a veil over my head before I could even process everything. It was happening so quickly, but I loved it anyway.

I would remember this forever for the rest of my life.

I was afraid of clowns, so when he touched my arm, I screamed, making my family and friends laugh.

But when I looked up, my heart dropped.

It was my idol Hayden Gray, smiling and removing the red rubber nose from his face.

Then I looked at Ryder in shock, to everyone's amusement.

"What?" I said, stunned and shocked that he had gotten *the* Hayden Gray to officiate *my* wedding. "I can't believe it."

"Believe it, my love, because we're about to get married," said Ryder, smiling at my shocked expression.

I took a few deep breaths and turned back to Hayden.

"I've always been a fan," I said. "This means everything to me..."

"I am honored to officiate your wedding, Miss Lacy," he said. His voice was husky-sounding and deep, just like his songs. I looked back at Ryder, and I could sense a bit of jealousy rising from him, but he kept it down with a smile. "Let's get this wedding started, shall we?"

"Yes," I said, nodding.

My heart was nearly bursting with all the love in the world for my men. Adrian looked happy as he stood before me, eyes glowing with excitement. Lucas looked serious as he gazed at me, and my heart pit-pattered in excitement. Cooper smiled gently at me, and when I looked at him, he winked, and my heart fluttered again.

"Ladies and gentlemen! We're gathered here to celebrate the union of this beautiful omega to her hunky bodyguards," said Hayden, and we all smiled as the audience chuckled. "I understand that the men have prepared their vows in advance. Why don't you go first, Adrian? You're the youngest and...possibly her favorite." Hayden winked, pulling more laughter from the crowd.

Adrian cleared his throat, and I smiled kindly at him. He looked nervous, his face wet from the rain, which thankfully stopped. His cheeks burned bright red as he held a paper between his hands.

"Lacy," he began. "From the moment I saw you, I couldn't bear the thought of leaving your side. You may think I'm reckless, but you help me balance that. In your presence, I'm calmer and more fulfilled than I've ever been. I love you, babe."

My smile grew wider, and tears came down my face. I loved Adrian with all my heart, and I couldn't wait to tell him when it was my turn to speak. His eyes roamed to my lips, and I shook my head slightly so he knew that we needed to wait until after the ceremony. He gave me a lopsided grin, and I blushed.

"That was beautiful," said Hayden, his voice catching. He pretended to blow his nose, but it squeaked instead. I rolled my eyes, and Ryder smiled. But I took a deep breath, instead taking it in as a memory I wanted to cherish forever.

"Lacy," said Cooper. "You inspire me, baby. Your love of music and everything that goes with it inspires me to chase my dreams, too. Not only that...you bring light and happiness to my soul, especially when we sing together."

I wanted to kiss him so badly right now, but I restrained myself until the very end. My tears were practically flowing by now, and a carnival worker quickly handed me a napkin.

"I've never felt as strongly for someone as I do you," said Lucas, holding my hands in his. I breathed deeply, relishing the roll of his deep voice over me. "Since the moment I saw you, I knew you were mine, sweetheart. I can't wait to grow our pack with you. Our omega and our jewel."

I swallowed. It meant so much coming from Lucas. He was always so quiet, and I thought he secretly didn't want me as his omega, so it was reassuring to hear this. Next, Ethan took my hands in his large, warm ones.

"From the moment I met you, my heart knew it had found its home. With you, I promise to love and cherish you every day for as long as we both shall live."

Lastly, it was Ryder, and my heart was literally beating out of control at this point.

"Lacy," said Ryder, his gaze fully on mine. "Today, we choose you. From the moment I met you to the day I thought I lost you- you've constantly been on my mind. Every morning when I wake up, I think of you. I promise and promise on behalf of my pack that we will protect you until death do us part. I promise to cherish you every day and choose you for all the days to come."

My tears came down freely as I absorbed every word.

"Lacy, would you like to say something to your pack?" asked Hayden. "Before I proceed."

I nodded.

"I never thought in a million years I'd find a devoted pack like you all," I said, my voice shaking with emotion. "In the past, I've been hurt, and I refused to open my heart. But when I met you, everything changed. There is something in my heart now. A light in my soul that I can't explain. I love all of you."

Ethan sniffed, and Lucas wiped his eyes at my words. I tore my hands away from Ryder to wipe my tears again. I could hear sniffling from the crowd, too. Gosh, I never expected to cry so much like this on my wedding day.

"Do you, Lacy of the Westwood Pack, vow to cherish and love Ryder of the Silverthorne Pack? Do you take all five men to be your lawfully wedded husbands?" asked Hayden.

"I do," I said, nodding and biting my lip. These five men would be my husbands in less than a minute, and my life would be forever changed.

"Do you, Ryder, take Lacy as your lawfully wedded wife? To protect and cherish until death do you part?"

"I do," said Ryder in his unwavering voice.

With a mischievous glint, he declared, "By the power vested in me, I now pronounce you husband and wife. You may all seal your love with a kiss!"

The crowd erupted in applause when Ryder and I leaned towards each other. He grinned at me, and I smiled back. He kissed me gently, pressing his lips over mine in a quiet passion but full of intensity he was waiting to give. Butterflies swirled in my stomach as he kissed me, letting the world know I was his.

I kissed each man in turn, and Lucas prolonged the kiss the longest- to the cheers of everyone. I pulled back, blushing but excited to be a married omega now. Colorful confetti cannons went off, showering us with a cascade of paper hearts.

Ben and Ty put on a final Electric Rose performance of the night for me, and I watched them teary-eyed and shocked they did this for me.

As we walked back to the limo, hand in hand, the circus performers and acrobats formed a joyful procession, dancing and celebrating around us. I was overwhelmed but pleasantly surprised at everything my men put together so fast for me. The circus music played, and the atmosphere was filled with laughter and happiness. My life had taken a whole new direction that I was whole-heartedly prepared for, that I'd denied myself for years.

I was ready to be an omega for a pack who loved and cherished me.

Thirty-Six

LACY

W hen we got home after our impromptu wedding, I carefully set my tiara on my bedroom dresser. The men were sitting in the massive jacuzzi in my house, waiting for me to show up.

But I needed a couple of minutes to myself first.

I had to process everything that had happened, and my new husbands respected it. Ryder had told me to take all the time I needed. I leaned against my dresser, staring at myself in the mirror. My makeup was all smeared from the rain and happy tears. My ruffled pink skirt was muddy and gross.

Making my way into my bathroom, I quickly stripped down and washed all the makeup off.

It took a few minutes by the time I finished. After being out in the rain, the thought of a warm jacuzzi sounded nice, and I was already missing my men. I wrapped a towel around my naked body in my lonely bathroom, cold and shivering as I walked out. I headed downstairs to where the jacuzzi was and found the men playing checkers in the middle of the water.

When I sauntered in, their eyes turned to me hungrily.

"She's here," said Lucas under his breath. I blushed and

dropped my towel to the floor. I swallowed as I felt their eyes feasting on my body.

"You're so fucking beautiful. Why don't you come sit on your alpha husband's lap?" said Ryder, patting his thigh in the water. I pursed my lips teasingly and crossed my arms over my chest.

"You didn't even get a chance to look at me," I said.

"Your alpha wants to touch," said Ryder. "Come here before..."

"Before what?" I said, my breathing quickening.

He tilted his head to one side as I stepped into the jacuzzi. Something inside me wanted to get punished, like the night I went to the haunted house. It felt wrong, but I wanted to piss him off again somehow. I hadn't forgotten how turned on I was that night.

The warm water hit my cold leg, and I sighed in wonderment. It felt so fucking good. Ryder pulled me onto his lap, and I leaned my head against him, relaxing as the water washed over me. His hands curled around my waist, holding me against him possessively.

Cooper floated to my right and Adrian to my left as they both grasped my breasts on each side.

"So plump," breathed Adrian, squeezing my breasts and kissing my nipple. "Could you be pregnant?"

"No, I'm not," I said a little too quickly.

Ryder's hand slipped between my legs, cupping my bare pussy. He pressed a finger into me, and I held my breath with anticipation.

He swirled his finger inside me while the two men sucked on my breasts. Cooper and Ethan massaged my thighs, opening me up wider for their pack leader.

"It would be nice to fill her with our babies," said Ryder to his pack, curving his finger inside me, and I was about to pass out from my arousal. "I believe it's time we consummate this sacred marriage."

"I agree," said Ethan, squeezing my thigh. My heart pumped in my chest as the men released their hold on me, and Ryder lifted me up with him out of the tub. He grabbed a towel and wrapped me in it while leading me towards the large guestroom bed. I quickly dried off my legs and stomach before he plopped me onto the bed.

∼

Ryder

LACY LOOKED disappointed when I walked away from the bed and sat on a chair facing her.

I wanted to watch her get mated by my entire pack first before I would seal the union. She looked so cute and bewildered as she watched me from the bed after I dropped her into it. I placed a towel underneath me so I didn't get the furs from her chair stuck onto my ass as I sat on it.

"Adrian and Cooper, make love to our omega first," I ordered. Adrian's lovemaking skills and Cooper's gentleness would ease our omega into our wedding night and make her more pliable-before I assigned Ethan and Lucas next, who were rougher. I've observed them during her heat and had it all planned out for her perfect wedding night.

I leaned back in my chair, watching Adrian sit up against the headboard, pulling her over his cock. She looked back at me at first, and I winked, enjoying how she innately sought the permission of her pack leader even though she didn't know it yet. But I knew it. And I would make sure she knew who her true alpha was after I allowed my pack to take her tonight.

I watched as she lifted herself over Adrian's cock, which disappeared into her wet little pussy. The way she licked her lips in satisfaction sent my cock upright, and I gripped it between my fingers as I watched Ethan and Lucas play with her breasts while she was penetrated.

Cooper had spread her ass cheeks apart and then pressed his

finger between her ass. Running his finger up and down as she twitched over Adrian's cock. Her thighs clenched when he pressed his finger around her sphincter. We had trained her ass well during her heat, and I hoped she was still used to it because she would get fucked in both ends tonight.

Twice-knotted with no mercy.

When Adrian bounced her on his cock, Cooper's pointer finger pressed into her tight sphincter going inside. She gasped, and my cock jerked in my hand. *Fuck.* My balls had tightened at the hot display of his finger inside her ass while her pussy was already full of cock. He kissed her neck and her shoulder as he pressed his finger deeper into her, inserting a second and third finger.

"Oh," she gasped when he stretched her with his third finger.

"I'm just getting you ready, sweetie," said Cooper. "Just let me take your ass tonight, and you will sing for me at the piano. How does that sound?"

"It sounds amazing," she said breathlessly while Adrian pumped himself into her.

I continued to watch as Cooper pushed his cock between her ass. Her widened eyes at the impact made me almost explode in my hand, but I had to wait until it was my turn.

$$\sim$$

Lacy

My HEART POUNDED hard as Cooper slowly slid into my slick-drenched ass. I was more than ready for him as I moaned against Adrian's greedy lips. Adrian made everything sexier and more fun with no pressure attached.

Adrian's finger slipped between us, and he caressed my clit with his thumb slowly at first. I gripped his upper arms tighter when I felt the rush of tightening in my pussy, as I got hornier. Cooper had pushed his dick inside me, stretching my ass wide as I breathed harder. I was still nervous, but I was getting used to being double-fucked at one time. It made me feel full and satisfied to the fullest.

"Your ass hole is clenching around my dick," said Cooper, kissing my neck and pushing my hair aside. He breathed in my hair. "Your fiery red hair turns me on so much, baby."

"She's hot as fuck," agreed Adrian, curling his thumb around my clit until I moaned. He rubbed me faster and faster, sending me to new heights. My belly clenched repeatedly, enjoying the feeling he created within me. I cried out as my pussy clenched around him. "I'm going to come too."

Adrian grunted loudly as he came after me, pistoning his pelvis further, pushing himself deeper into me to take his knot. Cooper roared as he came at the same time, too, his dick thrusting hard and fast into my ass. They both bit into my shoulder on either side, and I screamed. Bolts of electricity streaked through my body at their mating marks, and I orgasm around Adrian's cock once more as I shook and spasmed.

We lay content and spent on the bed.

I lay between Adrian and Cooper after the amazing sex we just had. Cooper played with my hair from the back while Adrian was still knotted into my pussy. My eyes were closed as I lay there, happy that I had consummated the marriage with at least two of the guys.

Adrian kissed my cheek, resting his hand on my neck.

"You look so beautiful with your eyes closed. When you smile," said Adrian. I opened my eyes, drained from climaxing twice in one session, and shocked I did it immediately the second time when they marked me.

"I'm trying to gather strength again for my next mating," I said, looking over at Ethan, who was combing his beard, preparing to take me next. Ryder was sitting in that chair, continuing to watch me- but with a studying, intense look in his eyes this time. "What are you thinking about Ryder?"

"If you'd like, we can give you a break and let you rest," he said, licking his lips. It looked like it was tough for him to make that call, and I understood where he was coming from. But I wasn't done yet.

"No, it's okay," I said. "I want this to be a real wedding night with you all. I'll just rest until Adrian's knot releases me. I promise."

"If you're sure," he said. "Because I'm not stopping mid-rut, even if you cry, honey."

I bit my lip nervously as my pussy clenched around Adrian's knot.

"I understand."

~

Ethan

THE OMEGA WAS FINALLY ALONE in the bed after Adrian's knot released her, and he left to go shower while Cooper went downstairs for a snack. I looked over at Lucas, and he nodded.

It was finally our turn to knot her. I had already mated her in the bath, but Lucas would still have the pleasure to mark her. As we walked to the bed, she looked up at me sleepily, her eyelashes long and lovely.

"We're going to take you next, beautiful," I said to her, turning her over onto her back. The pink indentations in her soft skin made my dick jump outside my bathrobe. I lifted her legs over her shoulder for our inspection. "Hold your legs up, honey, I'm going to take a look."

"Okay," she breathed, her face flushing pink like her pussy.

My heart pumped in my chest as I stared at her open pretty pussy. The underside of her thighs was covered in semen, and her labia glistened as Lucas spread them. I gazed at her pussy and ass clenching under my gaze. I gripped her ass cheeks and pressed them together. We watched the sticky cum from the other men seep down onto the towel underneath her butt.

"Do you see that?" I said to Lucas.

"She needs my baby in her instead," said Lucas, breathing hard, his eyes wild. "I want to take her pussy."

"You got it, brother," I said, my eyes not leaving the beautiful sight of the white trails marking her soft skin. "I will knot inside her ass."

"What?" she asked, blushing furiously. "Are you sure?"

"Yes, baby," I said, slapping her rump, and she gasped. Her scent was thick with arousal.

Just how I liked it.

Lucas laid on his back and pulled her over his cock. He sunk his cock deep into her pussy while I spread her ass cheeks apart. I looked at her ass hole, which was seeping in Cooper's semen. I couldn't wait to fucking knot her right in the center of her luscious ass.

Fuck.

My balls tightened as I spread her open like a feast before me.

"Hurry, Ethan," said Lucas, who was desperate to start pounding into her. Fucking her raw without any protection.

I pumped my cock and lined it up between her ass cheeks, slowly pushing into her wet small hole.

She arched her back, and I gripped her small shoulders as I filled her with my length. She was a petite beauty who looked even more beautiful with both of our cocks inside of her.

"Do you like that?" I whispered into the shell of her ear.

She nodded, her chest heaving in aroused breaths.

Lucas cupped her breasts, and I reached around to touch her clit while we thrust into her holes. Her anus clenched around my cock, hugging me to the hilt as I pushed and pulled into her. We were thrusting simultaneously into her as she rocked up and down, back and forth between us men.

Each pull of my cock from her tight hole caused my breaths to come in faster. I pressed my mouth on her back and neck, kissing her deeply as I pushed my cock deeper into her slick-soaked asshole. Our new wife was enjoying it by the way she dropped her head to one side, face flushed. My cock was heating up more and more with each bump and thrust. I rubbed her clit with my finger around and around until I could smell her scent rising to my nostrils.

Her sweet scent made my ball sack tighten every time.

"Fuck," groaned Lucas, gripping her hips and moving her back and forth between us like a machine. "I'm going to make you pregnant tonight, Lacy."

"Okay," she moaned, and at that moment, my cock exploded into her ass as I stilled. Lucas bounced her one more time on our cocks, coming at the same time. I swirled my finger around her clit faster and faster until she let out a small cry. She collapsed against my chest, her limp, warm body pressed against mine. "That was wild."

"It was perfect," I said, my cock swelling inside her as she slid off Lucas weakly. I lay behind her, massaging her arm while Lucas leaned over to her neck.

"I didn't get my chance, but would you like to be marked by me?" he asked her gruffly. She nodded and smiled. She cried out again when he bit her on top of her left breast, and I felt her ass clench around my knot in her arousal.

"I love you, Lacy," I whispered into her ear, my entire soul just for her. I wanted to protect her forever with everything I had and more.

She was ours. Our omega forever.

"I love you too," she said in contentment, allowing my knot to swell inside her ass. "I love you also, Lucas."

"I love you more," said Lucas, kissing her on the lips while I kissed her sweet neck.

"This wedding night will never be forgotten. I wish we could take a picture right now of my knot inside you," I said, and I chuckled when I saw her eyes widen with shock. "I'm just kidding, my love."

Lacy

AFTER CONSUMMATING my marriage with four guys, I took a quick shower before Ryder returned to the room.

He had left momentarily for a drink while waiting for Ethan's knot to release my ass, so I ran to take my chance before he could stop me from leaving the bed. I wasn't sure how he would react, but I was desperate to freshen up before the pack leader knotted me.

It was a big deal to me.

I squeezed the water from my hair and stepped out of the warm shower in record time.

The shower had woken me up more, so I was ready to get knotted again. The sweet ache between my thighs and the marking on my neck and breast reminded me of our consummation. I was smiling as I walked out of the bathroom wearing a clean towel, but I stopped smiling when I saw Ryder sitting on the edge of the bed, arms crossed over his hairy chest. His large muscular legs were naked, and his cock bulged angrily at me. The rest of his men lounged around the room, ready to watch their pack leader finally make our marriage official.

"I was expecting you in bed waiting for me," he said slowly, tapping his thigh.

"Sorry, I just needed a quick shower before..." I said, but he held a hand up.

"Come here," he said simply, and my heart pounded with arousal. All day, the tension between us was unbearable. He knew I wanted it, and I knew he wanted to punish me. The one night he spanked me has been on my mind ever since. I wanted it again, but I wouldn't say it out loud.

But an alpha knew his omega's needs.

"Why?" I said, slowly walking towards him. "Is it a bad thing that I wanted to clean up for you?"

"I wanted you here. Waiting for me and spread," he said, pulling my hand in his. Then he dragged me over his lap with my ass facing him. My heart pumped fast with excitement as I laid my head against the bed.

"I'm sorry," I breathed, even though I wasn't sorry at all when I felt his hand rub the back of my moist thighs underneath the towel.

"You're not sorry," he said, pulling my towel up and exposing my butt. "I can smell your scent. You're getting horny, little omega."

"I'm not," I said, trying to clench my thighs, but he quickly placed a hand between my thighs, separating them.

"Let's see how wet your pussy gets with every spank," he said. "Then I will rut you."

"What do you mean?" I asked nervously, but he lowered his hand with a loud smack on my right buttock.

I cried out at the impact of his rough palm against my skin, but it already had my pussy throbbing. He spanked me a second time on my upper thighs, and it stung more this time. I gripped the bedsheets. I couldn't help but feel slick seep down from my pussy now.

I smelled his alpha leather scent getting stronger with his dominance, and his cock danced against my hip with every spank. My ass burned, but it wasn't as bad as the first spanking I received from him. Maybe he was going easier on me because it was our wedding night.

"Your pussy is shiny with slick now," he said in satisfaction. My pussy clenched again at the thought of him studying me. "I'm going to take your pussy now. I need you to get on your knees and elbows. Okay, little omega?"

"Yes, alpha," I said, and that made his cock jerk.

I could see the hint of a pleased smile on his face as he watched me get into position on the bed. My back faced him, presenting my ass to him as I rested on my elbows.

"Adrian, suck on her right breast. Cooper take her other breast," ordered Ryder, and my pussy was pretty much dripping on the bed now. I ached for him to enter me and fill me up with his knot. I waited hours all day at the carnival. I envisioned it on the ride home in the limo, hot and bothered all the way here. "Lucas and Ethan, pay attention to her clit and thighs."

"Yes sir," said Adrian, quickly rushing over in his bathrobe, and he promptly laid on the bed under me, placing his lips around my breast with a wink. His tongue flicked my nipple, and my breathing accelerated. Cooper did the same on my other side, and when I looked down at both of them sucking on my breasts, my pussy throbbed and leaked.

I felt Ryder's thighs press up behind my own, and his enormous cock felt around the entrance of my pussy. He slapped his cock against my pussy lips, causing me to jerk with arousal.

Lucas quickly began rubbing my clit from the side, his large finger stimulating me even more. Every time I looked down at Cooper and Adrian, my pussy would clench hard. Ryder's cock began to press inside my pussy, and I stopped breathing as I took in all the feelings.

His cock stretched me out slowly, inch by inch, as he pushed inside of me.

"Her pussy looks amazing stretched out," said Ethan as he gazed from behind, rubbing my ass while he watched the pack leader rut me.

"She does," said Ryder, slapping my ass, and I cried out. "Let's make this marriage official, shall we, my beautiful wife?"

"Yes, alpha," I said breathily as he thrust inside of me. Every thrust had me shaking with desire, and my arms grew weak as he thrust powerfully into me. His strength was unmatched, his hairy thighs flexing against my legs.

Cooper swirled his tongue expertly around my left nipple, sending surges of arousal down my belly.

The pressure on my clit increased, and my pussy clenched harder around Ryder. Every thrust sent a shiver of arousal through my body, elevating my emotions to new heights.

"So tight, so delicious," groaned Ryder, thrusting faster until I could feel his swollen balls slapping against me. He was an alpha werewolf through and through, rutting me wildly as he gripped my hips to steady our rhythm. I arched my ass higher and felt the tip of his cock plunging deeper into me. It felt so fucking good.

He continued to thrust until he roared above me, climaxing deep inside me.

His seed flowed straight into my womb as he knotted me to him. Locking me to him until my pussy squeezed every last drop from him. Adrian and Cooper released my breasts with a pop.

I collapsed on the bed, and Ryder pulled me into a hug before I hit the bed. I pressed against his warm chest as he lay beside me, pulling me tight.

Our hearts were beating fast as one.

I could feel every beat of his heart against mine in the marital bed we shared. Finally, I opened my eyes and looked up at him timidly. I was pretty embarrassed that the spanking turned me on and that he knew it. But he smiled gently at me, stroking my hair out of my face. The other men were kissing parts of my body that I wasn't paying attention to as I tried to catch my breath.

"It's official," said Ryder, kissing me on the mouth. His hot lips against mine comforted my very being, and I kissed him back with all the strength I had before I would collapse into a deep sleep later. I was so sleepy from my big day but also full of love for the pack I was married to now.

"I'm an actual wife now," I said, unable to believe it. For so long, I'd sworn off mating a pack. Well, until the time was right.

"We're so fucking lucky you chose us," said Ryder softly. The men muttered their agreement behind me. I so badly wanted to turn around to kiss them all on the lips, but I was still knotted in deeply to my pack leader. This moment felt sacred and right. "You make me...whole."

"You do the same for me, too," I said, and we smiled simultaneously as our lips brushed together. "I love you, Ryder."

"I love you too with all my being, sweetheart. And one day, we'll see our little pups running around the house," he said, reminding me with a grin. I rolled my eyes, but I wasn't super opposed to the idea anymore. Plus, it was too late with getting knotted during my heat and all.

"Maybe in the future," I breathed. Ethan was pressing his ear to my belly and smiling. "Why are you smiling, Ethan?"

"Because the day might be closer than we think."

Sneak Peek of Freed by The Pack

Chapter 1
Olivia

I was laying as still as a statute this morning between two handsome as hell alphas assigned to me last night. One had locks of blond hair, and the other had short, curly black hair. I was scared to move and wake them up. Because if I did, all attention would be on me again.

I couldn't have that right now. Gosh, I needed a break from this breeding camp. Every day, I prayed I wouldn't go into heat, but I knew I wouldn't be safe forever. Once they matched me up to an alpha pack that I couldn't resist, then my heat would come in full force.

I knew it for a fact.

Suddenly, I heard shouts and glass shattering from across the hall. *Oh my god, was it fucking Lacy?* I shot up from the bed, and the two alphas stirred awake.

"Where are you going, Olivia?" one of them asked without a tone of grogginess in his voice. He was up and alert, standing behind me as I pulled my door open. My heart beat faster as I saw Lacy's room door wide open and a bunch of males crowding the

229

entrance. I heard her scream, and I rushed across the hallway before my alpha handler could grab me.

As I peeked in, I could see a window smashed open and alphas shifting into werewolf forms, jumping out the window. She fucking escaped with her pack without me. Lacy was my only hope out of here, and I thought she would care more.

"Let's go," the alpha told me, trying to grab my arm. But when I heard the gunshots outside, we all froze.

My heart sank with intense dread, and I wanted to throw up.

Was my cousin still alive? My alpha handler rushed out of the room, and I was left alone in Lacy's room as I stared out the window, trying to catch a glimpse. Heart pounding in my chest, I ran downstairs in my pajamas and to the front lobby.

Alphas in full uniform stood at the entrance with guns strapped to their shoulders.

"Go to your room," said Henry, grey eyes flashing as he paced the lobby. Then to his henchmen. "Make an intercom announcement for all omegas to stay in their rooms today. We have a situation."

Before I could argue or run out of the building, an alpha guard grabbed me by the arm.

"Please, my cousin is out there!" I screamed. "She could be dead right now. You don't want omegas dead, right?"

"If only you knew," he said, his lips turning up in a sneer, and then I knew that he couldn't care less. He shoved me into my room and closed the door without a word. I screamed and ran to the door, trying to twist the doorknob open.

He had locked it from the outside.

"Let me out!" I yelled, jiggling the doorknob.

I felt the familiar sense of depression weighing over me. It had disappeared when I saw Lacy in here with me, but now that she was gone, I wasn't sure if she had died or escaped. I rushed to my window and saw how high it was from the ground. I couldn't see anything except the ocean crashing against the shore of Howl's

Edge. Lacy couldn't be dead. She had to be alive. And for my sanity, I refused to believe she was hurt.

I'm sure she had escaped with the alphas. They were a strong group, and they were overprotective of her.

I paced around the room, jittery and nervous. Then an intercom came over the loud speaker we each had in our rooms:

"All omegas, please remain in your rooms. We will let you know when it is safe to leave. We have a situation. Once again, please remain in your rooms."

Hands shaking, I decided to make my bed while I waited until they released us from our rooms. I couldn't help the tears that flowed down my face as I pulled the pillows off. My family was probably worried sick about me now, but I hoped Lacy would tell them I was fine here even though I truly wasn't.

I lifted my pillow, and a small gray pill caught my eye. It was set perfectly underneath the pillow.

What the hell?

Remembering there was a camera in the room, I quickly snatched it while there was a disturbance going on and rushed into the bathroom. I opened my fingers, staring at the pill in the palm of my hand.

It was a heat suppressant pill. I quickly downed it, grateful to have some protection against my heat arriving. But the real question was...*who left it there*? I wondered if it was a total accident or if there was an alpha watching out for me.

END EXCERPT

Read the rest of Olivia's story *here*! Freed by The Pack

Author's Note

Thank you so much for reading! I appreciate you reading *Craved by The Pack,* and I hope you enjoyed reading the story as much as I had fun writing it.

I would appreciate it so much if you left a review letting me know your favorite parts of the story. This helps authors like me keep producing more stories for you.

To get updates on my next book and to get exclusive discounts, freebies, and sneak peeks, sign up for my newsletter below:

Newsletter

Tiktok: @laylasparks_author

Instagram: https://www.instagram.com/author_laylasparks/

Also By Layla Sparks

Howl's Edge Island: Omega For The Pack (COMPLETED Reverse Harem Series)

Book 1 (*Tiana's story*): <u>Stolen by The Pack</u>

Book 2 (*Keera's story*): <u>Auctioned to the Pack</u>

Book 3 (*Lyra's story*): <u>Princess For The Pack</u>

Book 4 (*Vanessa's story*): <u>Betrayed by The Pack</u>

Book 5 (*Jade's story*): <u>Matched to The Pack</u>

Book 6 (*Alana's story*): <u>Knotted by The Pack</u>

Book 7 (*Lacy's story*): <u>Craved by The Pack</u>

Book 8 (*Olivia's story*): <u>Freed by The Pack</u>

Dawn of The Alphas: Omega For The Pack Series

Book 1: <u>Maid for The Alphas</u>

Book 2: <u>Promised to The Alphas</u>

Captive After Moonlight Series: DARK Romance

Jenna gets a lot more than she can handle when visiting the smutty toy shop downtown. She looks for the perfect naughty toy, but little does she know that a werewolf is looking for *his* toy...

Now she's kidnapped by a psycho HOT werewolf who believes Jenna should be his.

Book 1: <u>Werewolf's Mate</u>

Book 2: <u>Werewolf's Captive</u>

Five Sexy Bigfoot Short Stories: Kink For Monsters

Book: <u>Five Sexy Bigfoot Short Stories</u>

Alien Erotica Series: Tantalizing Tentacles of Korynz *(short stories)*

Book 1: <u>Disciplined by My Alien Teacher</u>

Book 2: <u>Examined by My Alien Doctor</u>

Book 3: <u>Enslaved by The Alien King</u>

Made in the USA
Monee, IL
05 August 2024

02af7718-eedc-469b-af5e-399ee57bca19R01